Undisclosed Desire

2

I0451400

by Falon Gold

This is a work of fiction. Names, characters, places, and incidents either are the product of the author's imagination or are used fictitiously, and any resemblance to actual persons, living or dead, business establishments, events, or locales is entirely coincidental.

Text Nayberry to 22828 to receive updates

on new releases from *Nayberry Publications.*

Chapter One

Malisa Owens

Arrow, Colorado

If Apollo doesn't bring that helium tank and balloons, so help me God, I'll…

I can barely get to my feet on my own, so I don't know what I'll do if I catch up to Apollo, but I'm going to do something. I shift from side to side in Uncle Luke's recliner, trying to find a comfortable position for me and three baby boys. Each baby is already sitting on an internal organ of apiece. Not only have they made furniture out of my insides, it feels like they're having a contest of who can kick the hardest.

I'm spiraling into mind-numbing boredom waiting on their father to come back. Increasing desperation, for any entertainment besides the television, makes me wish for a member of my family to call from the gardens. It's located half a mile away from the house on forty acres owned by my uncle and his wife, Natalia, and should be fully decorated for mine and Apollo's wedding by now. In a year's time, Natalia will open the fifteen acres in the middle of the property to the public for events that'll be separated by barricades of lush shrubbery, which she personally planted and nursed for three years. If you ask me, The Owens Botanic Gardens are gorgeous enough to open now, with just the exotic flowers, angel fountains, and stone benches already on the grounds, along with the wide-open spaces. However, Natalia has her vision of her business, and well, nobody asked me.

Uncle Luke has already established an affluent horse-breeding company and riding school, where he gives horseback lessons on the far-left side of the property. As if that's not enough money for one household, Natalia works part-time as a botanist for the City of Arrow, and she's mother to my three-year old cousin.

How many jobs does a woman need? I ask myself, just as the front doorbell rings, *again.*

It's been going off since I sat down a few hours ago.

I answer it every time, regardless of the protests from my family. I need something to do, and they're too busy arguing about what will go where in the gardens. Therefore, the chiming echoes through the living area into Uncle Luke's man cave, where I lounge, are my entertainment.

I'm supposed to be resting my swollen feet caused by the triplets every time I stand up. I scoot to the front end of the chair in my robe. Hopefully, I'll be ditching it for my wedding dress soon. At least, I hope that I will. I'm going bat shit crazy in here, slowly.

I use the arms of the chair as leverage, pull myself to the edge. The tips of my nails graze my cell phone teetering on the end of the attached tray. I watch it land face down on the floor, and I'm not going to bend over and get it. That's unthinkable at this point in my pregnancy. Standing up and waddling around Luke Jr's playpen and toys strewn across the next room is not an easy feat either, but it's not as challenging as picking up the phone.

On my way to the door, I reminisce about how eight months ago I weighed a hundred and forty pounds and could see my feet. Now, I can't even imagine what they look like. Uncle Tommy says that I don't want to know either. Pillows and pin cushions are what he refers to them as whenever he's nearby, just to get a laugh out of everyone.

I reach the door finally, breathing heavily, opening it to another heavily pregnant woman with caramel skin, hazel eyes, and a curly mass of black hair. It curtains her tiny shoulders and teases the edges of her white summer dress that's pulling tight against her swollen breasts. Her eyes jut out of her head when she sees all two tons of me blocking her view into the house. She whimpers softly, and then her hands rise to her protruding tummy, as if she feels the need to protect her unborn child from me.

Damn, I've scared the lady.

"Hey, you must be Malisa," she says with a tremor in her voice, completely nervous. "Is Blake here?"

"Yes, he is," I pant, exhausted from the twenty steps it took for me to get to the door. "Would you like me to go get him?"

As if that's going to happen before night falls.

Her bright eyes roam the wraparound porch, as if she must think about her answer before she looks at me again with her mind made up. "No. I apologize for coming here unannounced, but he won't answer my calls… and he probably won't come to the door either. Listen, could you tell him that I'm pregnant? I don't want anything from him, but he has the right to know that his son will be born in another month."

Stunned, I stand in the opened doorway with my mouth sweeping the floor. Her eyes bounce around the deck again, landing on one of the pristine pieces of Natalia's white wicker furniture.

"That's it. Thank you." She whirls around, to shuffle away.

When she's getting into a dull blue, two-door truck parked on the circular driveway, my mind resets in time to register that she moves much faster than I can in my condition. Then, I recall that I forgot to ask what her name is. I'm sure Blake will know it though. Right after he tells it to me, he's going to explain how in the hell she knows my name and why I know absolutely nothing about her.

She looks familiar though, that's for damn sure! I'm going to have to get that phone off the floor anyway. Shit!

****

Astrid Daniels

A few minutes later

Oh my God, it's like looking into a mirror when talking to Malisa Owens. Seeing her for the first time in the flesh brought on birdbrain-itis. I'd come seven hours out of my way to Arrow just to forget why, but a painful kick to the inside of my navel fixed that moment of forgetfulness pronto. Baby Blake does not like being forgotten about.

It hurts even more that almost every member of his father's family has no inkling that he or I exist. I feel bad for those that are about to find out about us in such a shocking way. But what else could I do? Calling Blake, even as I was walking up to the front door of Luke Owen's ranch, got me nowhere.

Writing a letter or sending an email and text seems cold and detached, much like the government who issued me a badge at Arrow Sheriff's Department once. I no longer work for that entity, and hold myself to much higher standards when it comes to relaying events that will reshape someone's world, most times for the worse. Today is no different. Except, I'm a part of the awful circumstances, and boy do I appreciate not having to inform Blake of them up close and personal. He has nothing to say to me, and is probably going to hit the roof when he finds out why I'm back in Arrow.

I may have been spared that gruesome scene, but delivering the message to a face that looks so much like my own is just as traumatic. I couldn't stuff the double wide trailer I'm becoming in my driver's seat to get away from the ranch fast enough. The urgency to leave hit me hard as soon as Malisa opened the door, just like it did when I found out why my monthly cycle had packed its bag and absconded like a criminal six months ago. So did I a few days later, after bloodwork done during a doctor's appointment for a cure to the bug I'd come down with turned into a positive pregnancy test.

I detest surprises, don't subject others to them if I can avoid it, which is why I've been trying to contact Blake way before my planned visit today, with every intention to talk to him face to face. It only takes a small measure of kindness to ease someone into terrible news, which is exactly what the birth of our son is going to be for Blake. At least I'm not stressing myself out over him not answering his phone all thirty-two times I called, but it stings like hell, especially because it's my fault that he won't take my calls.

Nobody told me to fall in love with him or cut him off with no warning, playing a major part in the clusterfuck that my life and my first impression to Blake's family is right now. Now, every time I think about how much my child is going to have to do without because of my mistakes, the door to my emotions flings wide open. No matter how many times I board it up, tears push their way through while my chest implodes. I've been going through that since I moved… okay, ran away from Arrow.

What I wouldn't give for it to be the strange things that make a woman in my condition cry; it's warm outside, the wind is blowing inside the opened window, and the countryside is beautiful against the backdrop of the Sangre de Cristo Mountains. Instead, I'm swiping at blinding waterworks that stem from the one reason that would cause anybody's eyes to leak water; a broken heart.

Oh, and because you let yourself get knocked up by a man that didn't care to know more about you than the secrets of your body.

I do not need my conscious calling me out on my fuck-ups right now. I have enough to deal with, like not making the same mistakes twice. It's why I stood my wobbly ground at Luke's house long enough to tell Malisa what I should've told Blake a long time ago.

God, I probably looked more like a stalker to her than her mirror image, and what the hell, she's pregnant too!

I can only imagine what she's thinking of me, who'd stoop low enough to show up at a family function uninvited. I didn't even say congratulations on her wedding day or for the birth of triplets. No, in old-fashion creep style, I dropped a bomb, then left.

Well, it wouldn't have gone down like that if it wasn't much simpler to run back home to the people who love me the most rather than hit Blake with a grenade. I will not be apologizing for panicking and running. He and I don't, and never did, have a real relationship. It's a damn shame that I didn't let that stop me from wanting to be with him, often asking about his life outside of the job to get to know him better. I never got a straight answer from him, and yes, that's a big, flashing neon beacon with 'don't get involved, Astrid' or 'cut your damn losses and skedaddle, nut' written all over it.

The warnings are easy to ignore if you're telling yourself that your law enforcement career is all that matters, while not paying attention to what your heart is doing behind your back; giving itself away one tiny, unnoticeable piece at a time. It would be too late when I realize what is happening. The dynamics of our non-relationship would become as easy as breathing, and get me where I am today.

Nothing left in your chest and inflated around the middle.

Both are constant reminders of Blake, making it impossible for me to not want to see him again, even if it's for the last time. Nothing good will come of it though. Blake is an expert at making blissful ignorance seem like paradise, by always doing things that scream boyfriend to anyone listening. He just didn't want the title, and I didn't need him to own it when I had unlimited access to his body. The man makes love like a God, and my body refuses to let me forget it. If I'm not remembering how he fits perfectly inside me, I look down and see the evidence of him being there.

Yep, it's for the best that I follow the open road to my destination in the next state. If his piercing blue eyes meet mine, my fingers will want to run through his blond, military buzz cut. Mind-blowing kisses from his pink, full lips above his chiseled jaw line with cleft chin will follow next, dulling my good judgment. Truth be told, my intellect ceases to function whenever his wide shoulders and long legs move in my direction. Combine that with his uniform molding to his muscular body like a lover, the blistering touch of his large hands, and six foot two frame that never hesitates to curve around me, and I have a recipe for doing something stupid.

You're forgetting it's the formula for a baby and the taking of your heart, too.

It would be a blessing if I could forget, but I don't want my heart back. No man can hurt me again if I have nothing to give. Still, my watery eyes drop to the front of the gearshift, where an empty water bottle sits in one cup holder, my cell phone loitering in the other. It's not going to ring and I know it. If Blake cared anything for me, he wouldn't have let me sprint out of his life and stay gone.

Or contacted you by now. Answered your calls. Yet, your hope springs fucking eternal, doesn't it?

Absolutely! But hope is just another ingredient for the makings of a disaster between Blake and I. Determined to evade that at all costs, I press the gas pedal down to floor.

Chapter Two

Blake Powers

A few minutes earlier…

Vibrations in my front pocket drag my attention to my cell phone. I haul it out, checking the screen. Astrid Daniel's name is sitting plainly on it. I swipe the ignore icon, have been doing it all week. After shoving the device back in my jeans that I'll change for a penguin suit in a few hours, my gut churns for the umpteenth time today.

Something is going to go wrong. I can feel it.

I've been silently dealing with the nagging feeling since I woke up this morning. It gets worse as I sit down one of the chairs for Malisa's and Apollo's wedding, a little too roughly. I side-eye the closest eight-foot wall of bushes with lavender blooms that's separating the ceremony area from the reception. I resist the thousandth urge to sneeze and leave. I stay to make sure that whatever bad happens today doesn't get completely out of hand.

When this day turns sour for Malisa, and it will, she'll probably get hurt by it. Eighth-month pregnant women cry about everything. If she does, somebody isn't going to make it to tomorrow. She's my sister in all the ways it counts, even though we're not blood related, and no one's allowed to damage her heart in any way. God forbid it's one more of my secrets that comes out and ruins this day for her. The last traces of my boyhood crush on Malisa being discovered by Apollo almost a year ago almost did ruin things between them.

That secret wouldn't have come out if he didn't need to be taught a lesson for breaking her heart. She's always been beautiful, even when the full power of her attractiveness is hidden behind ponytails and glasses. I've always been a red-blooded male with 20/20 vision and a good degree of intelligence.

Well, *I* think I'm smart, or I'd have chased her romantically when we were kids. Because having no shared DNA between us left nothing to stop my lust, which developed way too damn early if you ask Malisa's mother, Lydia Owens. I call her Mama O. She's my mother adopted by the heart. I'm not going to lose her for anything, but I'll have some serious explaining to do if she or anyone else in the Owens clan ever finds out about Astrid Daniels.

The tossing of my insides morphs into full-blown heartburn, and I'm only thinking about trying to explain why I secretly slept with Astrid, who can pass for Malisa's sister, for months. Talking to Mama O about anything is damn near impossible; she makes a federal case out of just about everything. She can be completely overbearing too, until she's satisfied that her kids' lives are in order again. Poor Malisa just went through enough of that for the both of us, with just trying to convince everyone that Apollo is good enough for her.

However, the resemblance between my sister and Astrid alone will make Mama O *and* Malisa both poke their noses in my affairs. That's why I never introduced Astrid as my girl to anyone. Technically, Astrid can't be called my girl. We have a silent understanding about where we stand in each other's lives; no strings attached. Now, I have doubts about whether she really understood that, or she'd still be here with me. Right?

I sure as hell have no clue. Lucky for me, Malisa isn't complicated, already knows what she means to me, and is extremely happy that I only felt a light itch for her way back when. I still remember the big smile she gave me earlier this year when I told her that I wasn't willing to scratch that itch and that it never was that serious to begin with. Her obvious happiness about it would've hurt my feelings if I didn't love being her brother more than any itch I get. It takes a special woman to be glad that a man only felt a light attraction to her.

Well, Malisa's that special, and even a hormone-raging teenager can recognize a good girl that'll grow into a good woman. I'd like to say my testosterone has leveled out since growing up. It hasn't, but my gut-wrenching hunches are how I know Malisa won't be thrilled with me when she finds out that I didn't tell her the whole truth about why I'm still single. Letting her meet Astrid will expose my half-lies.

I'm not willing to be a part of that conversation, yet. Hell, I'm having a hard time with just being attracted to Astrid, who I haven't seen in six months. Talking about how bad it ended between us is off the table for now. It'll tear me apart, because she's disappeared, without a 'see you later sucker' or putting in two weeks' notice, just as bizarrely as she appeared out of thin air in my sheriff's department two years ago. She was ready to go to work. I hadn't hired a new deputy, didn't need one because I didn't want one. My perfect eyesight, a phantom abdomen punch that took my breath, and fully-functioning male parts made sure I knew I had a much bigger problem than unwanted personnel standing in front of me.

It's safe to say that I wasn't ready for Astrid. She's the version of Malisa Owens that's actually meant for me and even more beautiful than my sister who's the perfect girl to measure the perfect girl for me against. I just didn't expect them to look so much alike. Matching temperament and frame of mind would've been good enough for me.

Despite being everything I want in a woman, Astrid's timing couldn't have been more off. What's worse is having no matching DNA with her too, to stave off my attraction to her, and having too many personal problems to romance her properly. Blood ties would've saved me from adoring the craziest shit about her; she's just as bullheaded and independent as my sister is. Both have the habit of taking off and staying gone, too.

"What man would love any of that about a woman, Blake?" I ask, criticizing myself under my breath, which catches in my damn lungs when my words sink in.

Who said I love her?

I groan, "*You* said it, jackass." Then, I line another chair up and let it drop in place beside another one.

Talking to myself and catching on to my feelings too late is only a few of the unusual things that I've been doing since Astrid ghosted Arrow.

17

That's why I definitely wouldn't have employed a distraction that she would prove to be. It's common knowledge that I have no plans on hiring anymore employees as long as I'm elected sheriff, which is why I didn't get a heads-up from the county council that Astrid was coming to work for me. Or I'd have produced a valid and legal reason to keep her off my payroll, avoiding an expensive discrimination lawsuit that she surely would've won.

Obviously, falling deeply for a woman before she can say she's reporting for duty doesn't meet the requirements for not getting the department sued. Neither does being able to work two shifts, six days a week. My only deputy, Copper Miles, who came with the job, volunteers for double shifts on Sunday, gets out of going to church with his wife and three kids, but he gets home at five every day. It doesn't matter that I keep a family together, despite their religious differences, maintain the peace by using my workaholic tendencies to get out of family dinners with my parents, and dodge getting up every morning since I'm not an early riser.

None of those points work for the city council, who have the power to appoint extra manpower... make that woman power, whenever the hell they feel like it.

I suspect my parents have something to do with the council's decision that brought Astrid into my life, a decision which backfired in my *face*. They needed an excuse to free up my time for their own purposes. Rising car thefts and burglaries during the tourist season, along with a seventy-eight-year-old hotelier on the edge of town who doubles as a nuisance caller, works in their favor. Mr. Lindsey has the ear of every official in my county and gets spooked at every creak and squeak around his building.

No agency has enough officers to cover his calls, and the council members agree with me. Yet, they conspire with Arrow's influential citizens to fill empty deputy positions anyway. My world has been twisted up ever since they started that crap. Another chair plops out of my hands and down onto the thick grass.

"Go easy on the furniture, Blake!" Uncle Tommy yells across the lane between the bride's and groom's side. "They're rentals. Your Uncle *Luke's* wife's rentals. I told you he's a grumpy ass bear today and Natalia hasn't given him his porridge. You only have one star to throw at him, Sheriff. It doesn't have pointed edges to stick in his ass and slow him down while we run, and you don't have your gun. Do you really want him on our asses right now?"

As always with the self-proclaimed comedian who deliberately missed his chance at fame to make sure his family has plenty to laugh at daily, Uncle Tommy gets a chuckle out of me. "Sorry, Unk."

Tommy's brother, Uncle Luke, is definitely someone I don't want to tangle with about his wife's event equipment, even if he's all bark and no bite when it comes to his family. Still, I stop using unnecessary force with the lilac-covered banquet chairs and walk to the outer edges of the area where more seats wait to be put in place. I reach for one. My mind picks right back up with my first-time meeting Astrid.

After she showed up on my shift two years ago, well, the evening one, I slammed my office door right back closed. Then, I rushed to my office phone to harass every city council member on my speed dial until I found out who hired her. All thirteen, gray-haired members did. I demanded they send her right back to wherever she came from. But all Astrid's clean background, five years of experience with no incidents on the job, and a superb recommendation from the sheriff in Harrison, Utah got me was politely told to shut the hell up and deal with her.

If Karma is truly a bitch, she'll stick every man on the council in a cruiser with Astrid, while her uniform is fitting her curves like latex and that hypnotic jasmine scent is wafting off her flawless skin. Nothing like shared agony to make someone appreciate your point of view.

For six months, I seriously considered standing on my head every day during patrolling and training with Astrid, just to make my blood rush north instead of south for a change. The constant erections her presence causes are like a sickness. They plague me even when she isn't around. There's only so much *illness* a man can take before he goes looking for the cure. Astrid fell into keeping our office romance on the low without me having to say the actual words. Her reputation always being at stake in any world where the good old boys rule is motivation for being tight-lipped about sleeping with her boss. Our first time wasn't anywhere near a respectable bed but on my desk during night shift. I would've waited. She couldn't. Copper and the department's receptionist, Meagan Long, had gone home hours before.

The janitor's closet next door to my office would become the place to rendezvous during Meagan's lunch break, a single-mom that hates being away from her four-year old daughter. Any chance she gets, she's out the door to check on her at her mom's home ten minutes away. Astrid and I take... *took* advantage, but it takes one time to learn that Astrid is a screamer. I've been lying about having rats in the station ever since.

Lying, I hate it *and* the regrets I have for not giving Astrid her own shift after training her, but I just couldn't bring myself to do it. A lone woman on duty doesn't sit well with me. It would be nice if I could blame someone else for what went left between us. I have no actual proof that something's wrong, but something's damn sure not right, or she wouldn't have said goodbye to me without saying goodbye. Since I made the decision to not keep my hands to myself without thinking about the consequences, whatever it is, is all on me.

Don't forget how you wanted her close at all times, too.

If I hadn't, things would've worked out better for us both. I'd have my whole heart. She wouldn't have taken pieces of it with her after she suddenly quit a year later, but she should've confiscated it all. What's left just reminds me that there's something missing… and someone.

The phone vibrates in my pocket, again. I stand in place, balling my fists in the material that Mama O and the wedding planner tossed over the chairs only an hour ago. This is how I spend the few moments it takes to ignore a call whenever my sixth sense tells me it's Astrid, but I want to hear her voice so damn bad. I worry if she's okay, but the woman is tougher than I am mentally, almost physically too. She has to be one of the best in our profession, or some bigot would've used her weakness to force her out of uniform.

For now, she's not working anywhere and living in Harrison, Utah with her parents. I'll catch pure divine hell from her when I go there to get her back. She's means too damn much to me to just leave blowing in the wind, but I'm not going to answer her call right now. Yes, that sounds insane when I want her back badly, but insane is how I've been feeling since she split and started calling out of the blue, so I'm almost used to it.

Every time the phone rings, I think about the way that she blew out of town, and I take a vicious blow to the midsection. Talking to her on the phone is inviting her into my life to leave all over again. Somehow, I know that's exactly what she'll do, and I can't handle that. I'm not going to let her go next time, but her absence is making life less complex for me right now. She's one less person for me to have to choose over my parents who've been pressing me to become a true Powers every chance they get.

First, I must find a way to explain that I felt attracted to Malisa too many years ago to count, but that doesn't make Astrid a replacement. They look that much alike, and someone will mention it to her. Arrow is a small town. Everything is noticed by somebody. Most people don't have anything better to do than make a mountain out of a molehill, like Mr. Lindsey for instance. Nothing is ever truly a secret here, the woman's resemblance no more than a freakish coincidence. Still, Astrid deserves an advance notice before I make her truly mine. Trust me, I know women. Astrid will want to know about this before I ask her for her hand in marriage.

That's only one other problem that's eating at me. My parents are the much bigger other, and I don't know how I'm going to resolve it.

They're relentless with their demands for me to take over the businesses only run by Powers. Astrid deserves better than a man who can't put his parents in their place simply because they gave me life and one of them could be feeble enough to die if I say 'No, but thank you' to stepping in their shoes. I'd rather steer clear of their shoes and them altogether, and I sure as hell don't want to drag someone else into this mess.

Astrid did herself a favor when she left me, and she should stay away. Well, for now anyway. My instincts swear a confrontation with my parents is coming soon, and it'll be brutal. They'll make her life a living hell just because she's in mine, so I'm letting all her calls go to voicemail until it's over.

When I place another chair semi-softly on the ground then slide it over, knocking its seat against the next one, Uncle Tommy hisses from a few feet away, "Blake! Luke is bear with no porridge. You sheriff with no weapon. Stop it, dammit!"

Thoroughly chastised at twenty-seven-years-old, I murmur, "Sorry, Unk… again."

My parents can be just as grumpy as Uncle Luke, when they don't get their way. Just imagining spending time with my mother in an exotic location after Colorado's winters aggravate her arthritis makes me cringe. Running the family ski-resorts spread throughout the state with my father breathing down my neck will be a headache. Mingling with them and their like-minded friends at fundraisers for various charities damn near makes my skin crawl.

Mostly snobs attend the functions started by my parents twenty-one years ago, when my oldest sister succumbed to cerebral palsy right after birth. I was seven when some damn good luck on my end made sure that an invitation was sent to Mama O and Pops. Who knows where I'd have ended up if they hadn't come? Being raised with Malisa saved me from becoming a delinquent, just to get my parents' attention.

When I got comfortable with never being their first priority while preparing to enlist in the military, Ashley and Martin Powers approached me about taking over the day to day operations of their businesses. Suddenly, they remembered that they had a son and an heir. That caused a big fight between us. I'd always felt like sloppy seconds to their lifestyle up to that point, and I didn't give a shit that my idea for my future was beneath a Powers as far as they were concerned. I told them so. My father gave me a choice, the front door or the throne at the head of the Powers. My plans for moving out in a few months bit the dust. Joining the army, becoming a military cop, and getting a criminal justice degree happened much sooner than I wanted it to. I was really looking forward to the debauchery I'd planned for the summer after graduation.

Ashley and Martin Powers' interference with my life doesn't stop there. My father's stroke three years ago brought me back to Arrow. He never misses a chance to remind me of how he can drop dead at any minute because of 'mismanaging his health' or so he calls it, and my mother's inability to manage money. He stands up straight, walks, and talks as well he did before, so I'm convinced that he doesn't have one foot in the grave like he wants me to think. But it's planted in the middle of my world, threatening to push the Owens right out of it, and preventing me from creating what I want the most with Astrid, a family of my own.

Avoiding the third generation of Powers in Arrow that immigrated from Italy is a fulltime job. Taking over their obligations will eat up my spare time and ties to everyone outside the Powers' circle. Since I feel a tiny amount of loyalty to my parents, the struggle not to choose between them and someone else is real. When I do pick, someone is going to be in pain. Hurting feelings is enough to keep me off-balance and away from the one woman who was more than a secret lay to me before she ever took off her uniform.

Luckily, she's focusing on her career not settling down, which is the pits for the animalistic part of me that wants to bite her neck and roar *mine* to any man in a hundred-mile radius. But I have a little more time to set things straight here before I put all my efforts into convincing her that I'm the one for her. She's not going to be career-minded forever. I don't know how much longer I can go without her. Speaking with her now would be torture, so I don't.

A buzzing sensation skips down my hip again. A dull ache forms in the middle of what's left of my heart. The slice of a blunt-edged machete, instead of a razor-sharp one, cuts my intestines wide open, so it's not Astrid who's calling. It is bad news though. I pull the phone out. Malisa Owens' name screams at me from the display.

"What's wrong, Lisa Poo?"

"Blake, get your ass to the house right now and stop calling me Lisa Poo! You know I hate that!" she screams for real, completely distressed.

I panic and run down the path beside the groom's chairs that I've been manhandling. "What happened, Malisa? Is it the babies? You need to hang up and dial 911. I'm coming. Apollo!"

Apollo better be coming, too. I have no idea what end of the property he's vanished in, but he needs to get his ass to the house before I do. My duties consist of only getting him and Malisa through this wedding then settled in the monstrosity of a house that they're calling a castle resurrected thirty miles away, and make sure their babies have everything they need in the uncle-territory. Not the father's.

"No, it's not *my* babies!" she yells back. "It's *your* baby, you idiot!"

Feet begin to pound the ground around me. Thankfully, I'm not alone with whatever crisis is occurring in the house. I know absolutely nothing about delivering babies. One birth, I could figure out as I go, but three is just asking for something to go wrong today.

Just like I knew it would. Wait a minute. My baby? Idiot?

Since she's calling me names, she's not distressed but quite angry, and possibly delusional. I stop in my tracks, pretty sure I left some tread marks in the lawn. "What? I don't have a—"

"Yes the hell you do have a baby, Blake, and he just left the front porch with his mother that's still carrying him!"

Apollo, Uncle Tommy, Derek rocket past me on my left. My aunts Chrys, Jen, and Barbie race by on the other side of me. A golf cart barrels towards me from the opposite side of the property at a sensible rate of speed, with Pops driving. Mama O twists frenziedly in her seat beside him while shouting in his ear, "Go faster, Frank!"

He glances at her. "Sweetheart, I'm going as fast as it will let me. Calm down, or you can run with everyone else if you think you'll get there faster."

She leans back, raises her hand, and slaps him in the back of the head.

He should've saw that coming, even from behind. I did.

"Don't you tell me to calm down or run with everyone else, Frank! Something has happened to our child in the house!"

Pops reaches up and rubs the place she popped. "Lydia, I'm driving!"

"She's fine!" I shout at them. "Physically anyway!"

Mama O and Pops may not make it to the house alive to find out for themselves though.

"Blake, go find your baby mama!" Malisa screeches in my ear. "She's carrying precious cargo that's getting away!"

I look down at the phone, wondering has pregnancy cooked my sister's brain fully. "Malisa, what are you—"

"I'm talking about the woman that just left with your child that this family won't get to know if she gets her way!"

I huff, "Can I get a word in please?"

"No, you need to get in your damn car and get your son back here!"

My son! Yep, she's nuts, but something happened to make her this way.

I take a deep breath, and decide to approach this conversation from my patient sheriff's mode. "Calm down and start from the beginning, Malisa."

"Don't tell me to calm down and start from the beginning, Blake! If you were here, I'd knock the shit out of you! A woman that looks rather damn familiar by the way just left here, after greeting me by name at the door. She told me that she's been calling your ass to tell you that she's pregnant and your son will be born in a *month*! But she doesn't want anything from you. Then she left in a blue truck, real old-looking. Her knowing my name rocked me, so I forget to ask what hers is. I know I've never seen her in my life, but she sure as hell knows me. You will be clarifying why that is after you find her and bring her back here with the baby. Owens don't let their family slip away, Blake."

Malisa can't be all that crazy after giving me that much specific information. My mind starts to scramble back through it. I've only slept with one woman who drives a high-mileage Yukon Denali faithfully. She knows just enough about Malisa to recognize her, and she fits neatly in the time frame to have my child soon… and she could possibly be pregnant by me. We didn't always think to use protection when sleeping together.

"Astrid," I whisper, as things start to click into place. The calls, the pregnancy make sense. "*That's* why she's been calling me all week."

"Yes, Blake. Now, I have a question. Why didn't you tell me? We're family… and I didn't have to be pregnant by myself all this time," she ends on a whiny note.

Astrid's reasons for coming back aren't ideal. Missing the hell out of me and unable to stay away any longer would've been a better reason, love the best of all. The racing organ above my ribcage doesn't give two shits about why she's back, and insists that I don't let her get away again.

Something unfurls in the pit of my stomach. It doesn't take long to recognize it's a ball of stress unwinding slowly. I no longer have to wait to go to her. She's come to me. The situation could have happened under better settings though, and she didn't have to leave because she's pregnant. It's just more incentive to get my shit together.

"So Astrid's her first name," my sister snipes, completely pissy now. "It's pretty by the way. She got a last one?"

"Daniels," I answer distracted. "I didn't answer her calls, Lisa Poo. Not a one."

A wave of pain slams into my midsection and threatens to drop me to my knees. If Astrid wasn't hurt when she left six months ago, she is now. What woman who's trying to reach their baby daddy and couldn't wouldn't be hurt? It's fine when I'm in pain, but not when it's her, especially when I'm the cause of it.

"I'm sure you had your reasons, brother," she says sympathetically. Told you she's special. "Right now, you have a son that needs you and us, so go be the good man that I know you are and bring

Astrid and him back… but there's going to be hell to pay when you do." Now, she's threatening me. That's Malisa for you.

"I have a son with Astrid, Malisa," I murmur, terrified, shocked and thrilled. I have the family I always wanted, a lot sooner than I expected. Life is always doing its own thing.

"I know that!" Malisa snaps. "Now go get them!"

I will, when I find out where they are. The hair on my arms and neck stand on end. I fight not to panic while frozen stiff. I can't decide what to do next or which direction to follow Astrid in. "Fuck! Shit!" I start to turn in circles.

"Stop cussing at me and move toward your truck in the garden's parking lot, Blake! She's in a blue—"

"I know what she drives, Malisa." At least I know that much.

"Then why the hell are you still turning in circles?"

Because shit just got more real than I ever thought possible. Now take your own advice and calm the hell down, Blake, so you can think.

I stand still, take another deep breath, and channel Sheriff Powers again. My heightened emotions say fuck that and jump in intensity instead. I'm going to have to find Astrid while I'm a basket case.

"I can see you from the kitchen window, Blake! You're still here!"

I shouldn't be. "Which way did she go after you talked to her, Malisa?"

"She went back towards town."

"Okay, that's east, so she's probably heading back to Utah. How long has she been gone?"

"Maybe four minutes. It took me that long to get the phone off the floor." Enough time to cover four miles at sixty miles an hour. I have ten more miles left to catch Astrid before she reaches the highway.

"Malisa, I'll call you back."

"You better, big brother from another mother."

I let her do the hanging up, while I cross the three acres between me and my truck. Except, my feet are moving on their own because my head is spinning. I can't make sense of why life just had to intervene in my decision to keep sections of my world separated until I could lay to rest one thing and prepare Astrid for the other. I dare *anyone* to hurt her because of any of it though. It'll be the last thing they do.

Chapter Three

Blake

The best thing about being a sheriff is the sirens mounted on the dashboard of my personal vehicle. When they're on, even old people get out of the way quickly. Usually, there's no one to give a mini-heart attack to on the roads into town at this time of year, when Arrow is slow and quiet. The only vehicle I'll see will probably be the exact one I'm looking for.

When my speedometer clocks five miles in a minute, I start to worry if I'll ever find her. Nothing but asphalt stretches before me, until I crest a hill that drops like a rollercoaster. At the bottom of it is a blue truck that's going twenty miles over the speed limit. Now that I know why Astrid's been calling all week, I'm sure she's been phoning me from Harrison. Tracking me down in Arrow must have been her last resort.

She should've made plans to attend a wedding and meet both sets of my parents instead. They're going to be grandparents and have a right to know who the mother of their grandchild is. That's the only 'right' the Powers have, and they'll lose it if they start to pressure Astrid about anything. But, I have to catch her first before I can introduce anyone to her.

I mash the accelerator to the floorboard. The suburban shoots forward then chews up the half mile between me and Astrid in seconds. Her older model automobile can outrun most vehicles. I make sure of that with monthly maintenance that I do myself, well, I used to do it. It's good my truck comes customized with a hemi engine courtesy of the county, or she'd get away like she's trying to.

When her brake lights activate, I ease off the gas. She pulls over. I follow her over the white line to the soft shoulder. I'm barely in park when I open my door and jump out. In her rearview mirror, I see the uneasiness sitting plainly in her face as I walk toward her quickly. Her expression deepens a little more as I get closer to her door. I snatch it open. She leans back to look up at me. Her button nose scrunches up. Glossy lips tighten into a thin line above red-rimmed eyes. All signs that she's mad and possibly been crying. She's never looked more beautiful to me, and I need to see all of her.

She glares up at me through narrowed slits of her eyes. "What are you doing? This isn't how you perform a traffic stop."

I reach inside the vehicle, undo her seatbelt, and extend my hand to her. Her scent surrounds me and fogs up my head, as usual.

"This is not a stop, Astrid. Now get out." I can't get anywhere near her as much as I'd like to be if she's sitting down.

"What? No, Blake! If you're not pulling me over for speeding, I'm not getting out."

"Astrid, I don't want to hurt the baby, so I'd rather you step out on your own, but I'll get you both out safely if I have to."

She looks out of her windshield and rubs her hands down her bare knees. There isn't much of her lap left thanks to me. A mix of dread and excitement intermingle inside me. I'm responsible for another human being now. That number will rise to two if I get my way.

"Blake, don't do this," she pleads softly.

"Oh, I'm doing it, love, and I'm willing to use my authority to get it done, so out."

"I thought you said this wasn't a stop," she stalls.

"It isn't. You have to do this because I need you to as a man." I probably should've said as *her* man, but I don't know if she wants to hear that when she's obviously trying to keep her distance.

Her mouth snaps shut. She exhales heavily then places her palm against mine. As soon as she's upright, with one hand resting on the door through the opened window, I let my eyes roam down her front. The curvature of her face is slightly thicker, her advanced pregnancy crystal clear, and feet dressed in flip flops with a tiny bow. It's a miracle she has on shoes, because she doesn't wear them unless she has to.

Everything else about her seems to be exactly as it was the last time I saw her, except for the extra glint to her skin and her tummy that's almost swallowing up her slender frame.

My son is doing that to her body.

And baby Blake is already a big boy. She's taking care of him well without me, which makes me proud of her and unsettles me. I want her to be self-supporting. No storm will blow her over when it comes, but I want her to need me too. I'll shelter her from everything when I can. Obviously, that's not necessary. Thick emotions begin to clog my throat.

Astrid looks away. "I've said all I needed to say, so say what you need to quickly."

I find it troubling that she's avoiding my gaze. She doesn't do that either.

"Fine," I say hoarsely then take her chin in my fingers and turn it to me before tilting it up, just so my mouth can drop down on hers.

The distance between us is begging to be occupied, but I'll probably crush my child if I get next to her like I want to, like I used to. I settle for placing one hand in the small of her back. Her lips sit stiffly beneath mine. Just as I wonder if I've waited too late to give her everything that is me, she groans, and then opens her mouth to let me in. Relief swamps me. A heat wave ripples through my chest, overruling the uneasiness sitting there like a brick house. My stomach clenches beneath my T-shirt, pushing all the breath out of my lungs. This woman will probably always have this effect on me.

I open my mouth wide over hers, to drink in air. Her tongue slips between my lips and begins a war with mine. I never meant for the kiss to become aggressive, but it does, and Astrid is the aggressor. More sensations than I can stand bombard my center. All my blood whooshes south, until my jeans are being pressed outward by an erection that wants its freedom badly.

Her fingers tighten around mine, while her other hand glides across the nape of my neck, pushing through the closely-shaved ends of my haircut. A car honks its horn while riding by. The wind slaps at my shirt, reminding me of where we're at. I take one last swipe across her tongue coated with water and sweetness, and then step back.

Astrid drops her forehead in my chest, panting softly. "We can't do that again."

"Why?" I ask. Something tells me that I don't want to know the answer.

"Because we're not going back to your idea of a relationship."

"No, we're not, Astrid." Certainly not if I can damn help it, but I know what she meant; we aren't going any further than baby mama and baby daddy status.

I need to get her out of that headspace and in my territory to change her mind. To do that, she has to come home with me. "We need to talk about our future and the baby's before it's born. I know I have some explaining to do, but so do you. It's not safe to talk on the side of the road though. Get back in your truck and come back with me to the house. We'll talk there after my sister gets married, if my family doesn't kill me first."

She lifts her eyes to mine. Hers are filled with apprehension again. She's never been this anxious around me, and I don't like it. I prefer the brown-eyed, sultry look she gets right before we make love more.

"Blake, I wasn't invited to—"

"*I'm* inviting you to my sister's wedding. Malisa has already demanded that I bring you and the baby back, or there'll be hell to pay. Well, there's going to be hell to pay anyway for not telling them about you, but save me from the extra shit I'll be put through if you don't come back to meet everyone."

"You're not mad with me about... well, everything?"

I would be, but it's my fault that she thought she needed to leave in the first place and hide the pregnancy from me.

"No, love. I've never been more glad to see you."

"I didn't think you would be after I up and left then showed up here like this." Then she inhales deeply and squares her shoulders.

What is she bracing herself for? Maybe, she's not as sure about what will and won't happen next with us as she portrays. I hope not.

"You thought wrong, sweetheart. Now let's go before someone else comes along, like my family. They're nosy as hell and will come looking for us if we don't come back soon."

She arches one eyebrow. "Are you sure? I probably ruined your sister's day. Meagan told me where to find you, and she doesn't mind if I wait for you at the station with her."

"No." She's waited for me long enough. "I'm positive you haven't ruined anything. Malisa's more ticked off that she's been pregnant by herself. And, I'll be damn if I let you get out of my eyesight before I've told you how I feel about you."

Astrid curses under her breath then steps back. "Okay, I can do this," she whispers to herself. "I'll go with you."

She turns sideways, to get back in the truck, with me gripping her hand tightly. I don't want to let go. The rest of my fingers are spread wide behind her back. When she settles in her seat, I grab the doorframe and release her fingers unwillingly, to bend over, redoing her seatbelt.

She arches the other eyebrow, which is only inches from mine. "I could've done that, you know?"

"I unfastened it and I should fasten it back, don't you think?" Any excuse to be near her and my son will do.

I step back reluctantly. She closes her eyes, shakes her head, and grabs the steering wheel with both hands. Her grip is white-knuckled. She should get use to me making sure she's has what she needs, again. Yes, she could live without it, but I have six months of not doing it to make up for. I backpedal to shut the door. She starts the engine. I find it impossible to walk away.

Her head tilts to the side. "I'm not going to drive off in the other direction if that's what you're thinking." It isn't.

Astrid's word is her guarantee. I just don't want to take my eyes off her. Who knew that eyes could starve? Mine are gluttons for the sight of her.

"Even if you did, baby, I'll follow wherever you go."

She smiles for me, making it feel like old times and even tougher to move away, but I do. After swinging up into the suburban, I flip the sirens off, swerve around in the road then glance in my rearview. When I'm sure that Astrid's not having any kind of problems, I start back toward Uncle Luke's. Then I consider driving in the other direction myself, rather face a firing squad than go back to my family and their heartbreak that I'll cause when they learn I've excluded them from a significant portion of my life. Fleeing will hurt them even more.

I'm damned if I do, damned if I don't, always risking disappointing someone. My absentee parents. The Owens. Now Astrid. This has been my living conditions in Arrow for as long as I can remember. It's always something that I need to keep hidden or hope it goes away to minimize the collateral damage. Completely fucking nerve wrecking. Keeping the peace in Japan, where the martial artists are more lethal than a AK-47 during civil unrest, doesn't even compare.

Keeping pieces of my life divided and locked away isn't working anymore. They're spilling out into the light one by one, leaving me no choice but to be transparent with the everyone. That might kill my biological father. He'll never earn the daddy of the year award, but I'd rather not be the reason he's fitted for a toe tag. I can't be sure how my truth is going to affect Astrid though, and she's the one I'm worried about the most.

She may not want anything to do with me anymore after all the shit hits the fan. The blowback will be worse than a tsunami if some of the Owens decide to feel the same way. Well, Malisa is just going to kick my ass, but I could still lose everyone else that stood between me and the world when doing right by me was the last thing on the Powers' minds. Everything I am I owe to the Owens.

Hopefully, they'll just go up one side of me and down the other for keeping them in the dark about Astrid, and now baby Blake. If I'm lucky, Mama O will just bean me in the back of the head with the palm of her hand a few hundred times, then welcome Astrid and the baby into the fold. I have no doubts that she'll do the latter. It's the former I'll need to survive.

My truck conquers the miles to Uncle Luke's too damn fast for my liking, even while riding at the speed limit. The bottom of my stomach drops. I past the circular driveway in front of the house to turn onto the paved straightaway that leads to the parking lot for the gardens. Before I park between Aunt Chrys' red Avalanche with a gold grill and rims and Aunt Barbie's pink Impala trimmed in chrome, I strip my jeans of my phone to call Astrid.

She picks up on the second ring. "So, you do still have my number, huh?"

Her husky tone invokes memories that I also still have of me pushing into her too damn warm and moist body. As if I wasn't having enough troubles with the extra hard part of me already.

Standing on my head beside my truck becomes a possibility, but there's no time for that.

"Yes, I do, Astrid, and I'll tell you why soon. Right now, I need you to not park and give me a ride to the house, so Malisa can get another good look at you while I finish setting up the chairs for her wedding."

Astrid stops sideways behind my truck, with the windows rolled up, confining the can-cooled blast of her air conditioner. The atmosphere shifts around me as the line gets as quiet as the dead. Immediately, I know which gate to hell that I've opened unintentionally.

"You told me that your sister and I only favored, Blake, when I asked you about her, but it was like looking at myself actually." The one time she asked about my family, little snippets to describe everyone is all she got out of me.

"Yeah, she thinks you look familiar too, and I was vague about a lot of things I told you. It'll take the rest of the month to get through the details. I need your promise that you'll stay here with me until I've told you everything." I take the keys out of the ignition and turn the alarm on.

"Blake, I… I can't stay here for the rest of the month with you."

"Why not?" If she refuses to stay three weeks, I have no hope for getting forever with her, not in Arrow anyway.

"Because my life is back in Harrison now." So is the help with the baby that she thinks she can only depend on.

"You moved here once before by yourself, Astrid." Another thing she has in common with Malisa, who's come back home to stay after living in Utah for years. Hopefully, Astrid doesn't follow down that path too. If she does, I'm going right behind her.

"But you won't be by yourself this time," I promise quickly as I stroll between the cars.

"You work sixteen hours a day, Blake."

"Not anymore as long as you're here, and you know I have a whole group of people who are willing to hire more deputies if I want them. What's the next thing that's stopping you from giving me another chance to prove that I can make better decisions than I did two years ago?" Convincing her to stick around adds to the other insurmountable hills I must climb, but it's the only one I'm going to concern myself with right now.

I open the passenger door of her vehicle and get inside. She takes the phone from her ear, deposits it in the cup holder that she always leaves it in while driving. I stuff mine in my pocket. When she drives out of the lot without answering me, I don't press her to, for fear of running her off faster than she's already planning to go.

The silence thickens around us as she avoids my gaze that's pinned on her face. She finds the front of the house on her own, stopping on the far end of the driveway, but we're in bird's eye view of the front door. It opens. Malisa and half of the Owens spill out of it, onto the porch. I curse quietly, thinking about telling Astrid to keep going.

She giggles and shuts down the truck. "Even I saw that coming, Blake, and I don't know your family. It's okay if they want to meet me."

It seems we're going to have to take road trips every time we want some privacy, which I won't need if I can't get Astrid to talk to me or stay. I twist in my seat, facing her with my back to the window.

"I need you to promise me that you'll at least think about staying for a little while, so we can—"

"Can what?" She frowns. "We've done all we're going to do, Blake."

"No, we haven't. You're pregnant with my son, Astrid. We'll be doing things together for him the next eighteen years at least."

The bridge of her nose wrinkles up again, and lips compress into a thin line. "You couldn't even tell your family about me. Now you want what from me? A real relationship?"

Damn, she's pissy.

42

Understandable, but I need to get her out of that space too, by backing off.

"Yes, I want at least a platonic relationship with you for my son's sake, but I'd rather have you both," I admit quietly.

She rotates at the waist to face me, placing her back against the door and bent knee against the gearshift. "You didn't want more than casual sex with me until now. How am I supposed to believe that suddenly you're ready to commit and want a family?"

"We didn't feel casual to me, Astrid, and a family is what I've always wanted... with you."

I grow angry and turn it inward at myself—she wouldn't think she's a casual anything if I'd been more upfront with her about what she means to me. The strategy to not lead her on with sweet words of commitment worked too damn well. It doesn't mean that I didn't feel committed to her. Every day we were together, I tried to show it to her. My biggest sin will always be not telling her.

I swipe a hand across my jaw. "Sweetheart, I wasn't ready for lots of things when we met or for you to leave me behind. The thought of coming for you soon kept me sane. The stupidest thing I could've done was let you leave, but there are reasons why I seemed unready to settle down with you and a family and didn't answer your phone calls this week. That doesn't mean I don't think of you as my girl *and* my family. I have some shit hanging over my head that I don't want you getting twisted up in. I wanted to straighten it all out first, but the best laid plans... you know the rest."

She crosses her arms across her breasts, making them puff out of the top of her dress a little more. My jeans become a little more uncomfortable around my hips. I jerk my eyes up to her face wearing a glare when she should be happy.

"I'm not a child, Blake. You don't need to protect me."

"I protect, Astrid. That's what I do, and I'm damn sure going to protect the woman I love."

She gasps. Her eyes widen until they encompass her face.

I lean forward. "Put your eyes back in your head, love. You were hired to work a shift by yourself, and you never did. I have never stepped out on you or acted like you didn't exist when we weren't sleeping together. I worked on your truck, around your apartment as much as I did my own, and spent most of my days and nights with you. That should've clued you in on my feelings for you right there."

She grins, but it goes away as fast it comes. "Hell, I thought you were just keeping me buttered up, had great stamina, a high sex drive, and needed me around for whenever the urge for sex hit you."

A laugh bubbles up in chest. "When the urge hit me, huh? The same can be said about you. Did you forget you're the reason I have to lie to everyone at the station about the rats that don't exist in the janitor's closet? I was the only one willing to wait until we got back to one of our apartments to get you naked."

Her smile returns, and the sultry look I love to see on her face appears. Then both fade. It's like she doesn't want to feel anything around me.

"It's true that you never ignored me, refused me, or made me feel like I was being used while I lived here. That's part of why it was so easy to stay with you for a year when I wasn't really with you, but you didn't tell me how you felt or wanted me to know much about you, so I didn't assume you really cared for me. That creates… stalkers."

I'm not blind to the fact that she hasn't mentioned if she cares for me too (I can wait however long it takes for her to reach that point), or if she's already given up on me.

"No, Astrid, you assumed I *didn't* care. That's on me because I didn't tell you a lot of things that you should've heard from me, but you were always with me and I was always yours. I am sorry for every time you wondered about my feelings for you, and I'll fix that if you let me. Will you stay in Arrow until I prove you wrong about me?"

She opens her mouth. The shadow of a human form approaching from behind me falls across her dress. I'm surprised no one approached the car sooner.

"Don't answer me now, Astrid." If she stays here long enough for the reception, she won't risk driving and arriving back in Harrison after dark. Practical and reasonable should be Astrid's middle names, along with sexy even while pregnant, and too damn hot to handle in bed or against a wall…

Stop it, Blake, or you will be standing on your head for real.

I hold on tightly to the thought of getting at least one night alone with her. Hopefully, it's enough time to persuade her to stay for a lifetime. A knock on the window fires off behind me just as I reach down to adjust the swelling behind my zipper. Astrid's eyes track my movements. The top of her tongue peeks from between her lips. A throb pulses through my crotch. I lurch around to sit correctly in my seat before I pull her into it with me, push her dress up, and dive penis-first into her body with Malisa looking. Astrid has yet to deny me her body. I suspect her heart is another matter though.

Malisa stands on the other side of the raised glass, with her hands laying on each side of her stomach. She can't reach down far enough to get to her hips anymore. "You might as well get out and face me like a man, Blake."

War has just been declared.

My head swivels to the woman sitting beside me. "You know this is the last time you're going to see me alive, right?"

She laughs out loud. "I swear I'll attend your funeral."

"Seriously! You're not even going to help me?"

"Nope."

"Ain't that a bitch. I'm your child's father and you're just going to sit back and watch my sister murder me," I retort dryly.

"Blake's cussing, Mama!" Malisa yells out.

The front door slams shut shortly afterwards. Mama O is getting clear of the childish back and forth between Malisa and I, that is until she catches me alone to find out whatever it is she wants to know about my current situation. It's the same thing she did after Malisa arrived in Colorado with a broken heart, refusing to clarify what happened.

Broken is probably the same way Astrid returned to her folks, or scared to death.

My playfulness dies a quick death. Shame, from making her feel like she needed to look elsewhere for restoring her well-being, fills me and kills my hard-on. Well, I'm not thinking of groping my baby mama in front of everyone anymore, but I'll make up the last six months to Astrid if it's the last thing I do. I have to get around Mama O's black stare first. It'll come after she and Malisa get the dirty details of my relationship with Astrid, and they will get them.

I gain empathy for Malisa for what she went through when it was her wearing my shoes. You'd think she'd have some compassion for me. Nope, that woman takes advantage of payback every chance she gets when it comes to me. Okay, so I'll deserve whatever she does after all the pranks I've pulled on her and the trouble I've gotten her into, including putting her on the no-fly list when all she wanted was some space to get over the pain Apollo hadn't meant to cause her.

I reach over the seat and place my hand over Astrid's baby bump. "I wish daddy had gotten a chance to meet you on solid ground, little man, but my sister is going to make you an orphan first."

Astrid's stomach depresses, as if my touch is sucking all the air out of her. A hard lump the size of a golf ball rises under my palm, like our child knows the feel of my hand and sound of my voice. Butterflies begin stomping around my insides.

"Don't worry, Blake." Astrid pats my knuckles lightly with her fingertips, with a ghost of a smile haunting her lips. "He won't be an orphan. I'll still be here, and I'll make sure to tell him all about you... Won't I, baby boy?" She ducks her head and coos to the baby.

Watching her interact with the little person that's not even here yet makes a knot form in my throat. This is the Astrid I know; bright-natured and banting back and forth playfully with everyone. She's the only one who could make me forget all my issues just by being herself.

My mouth falls open, pretending to be appalled by her response, though my heart feels heavy. "Just telling him about me doesn't make me feel better, Astrid. Malisa is going to kill me about *you two*."

Astrid gives me a sympathetic smack of her lips. "Yeah, but the baby will be well taken care of after I get your pension and go back to work." At least, she'll get something out of being with me besides a whole lot of responsibility in the form of the mini-me rumbling around her body.

I flop back in my seat, grumbling, letting my hand falls in my lap. "You're waiting for me to die, aren't you?" I joke, but it'll serve me right if she really is—she uprooted her life because she didn't trust me to be there for her. There's nothing I wouldn't do to be able to go back and change that.

She shakes her head and snickers. My door opens suddenly. I glimpse up at Malisa, who looks even angrier than she sounded on the phone, with Apollo standing behind her.

"Out, Blake!" she demands. "You know I can't bend over to beat you properly or greet Astrid. It takes two minutes for me to get down. Two minutes to get back up. I know that for a fact."

With one hand, Astrid covers her mouth to suppress the laughter rocketing out of it and reaches for her door handle with the other one.

"Don't you dare," I hiss.

Her hands drop on top of her stomach. A snigger escapes from her lips. "Blake, I'm pregnant, not an invalid. You don't always have to open every door for me."

"We've had this discussion before a year ago, remember? The outcome will be the same. Yes, I do have to open every door for you, and no, being pregnant does not make you an invalid. You can still walk on your own *after* I open the door… if you want to walk. I *can* carry you to the house."

The corners of her mouth lift and stay there this time. "Thank you, but no thank you. If you're going to open this door, you need to do it quickly. I have to use the little girl's room every twenty minutes it seems lately."

Malisa groans and shuffles backwards into Apollo. "These kids act like my bladder is a chair too. I swear one of them is always sitting on it."

Astrid mutters, "Amen."

Apollo kisses the top of Malisa's head then wraps his arm around her stomach from behind. "It'll be over in a little bit, sweetheart. Then your uterus will probably say to hell with producing anymore children, and you won't have to go through this again."

Malisa sighs. "I sure as hell hope so, Apollo. As much as I'd like a little girl, I'd like to see my feet too."

"Not right now you don't!" Uncle Tommy yells from the front porch. He hears like a bat, even at thirty-nine-years old. Then his head rebounds forward, as if someone smacked the shit out of it from behind. Probably Aunt Chrys. She doesn't mind taking over where Mama O leaves off.

Chapter Four

Blake

I get out the truck and make my way quickly to Astrid's side, helping her out.

Malisa turns around to face Apollo. "I don't want to walk, babe."

He uses his long arms to reach around her and squeeze her ass, while grinning. "Okay, sweetheart." Gross.

She snickers and stands on tiptoe to kiss the underside of his chin. "Just kidding. I got all the way out here on my own. I can get back… before the wedding I hope." She steps around him and takes off at the pace of a turtle along the curving driveway.

When her hands flail out, like she's losing her balance, Apollo catches her waist in both hands from behind. "Wait, baby. Hold on to me. You really are unstable, aren't you?"

She snorts, stops, and lets him intertwine their fingers before moving forward again. Astrid rounds the back end of the truck, under her own steam. I wish she needed me to hold onto, but I certainly don't wish triplets on her or me just so she'll cling to me, so I walk a step behind her, praying for the day she'll reach for me on instinct.

Uncle Tommy steps to the edge of the porch. "How many babies is *she* carrying, Blake? Where did you and Apollo buy your sperm at so I know *not* to go there?"

Pops chokes on air loudly then coughs out, "Shut up, Tommy!"

"I didn't say nothing wrong that time, Frank. Come on, I have some sensitivity."

Aunt Chrys snaps her head around to Tommy standing beside her. "No, you don't. Never have."

"Yes, I do, and I did. You'll see when Derek knocks you up, Chrysalis, and you two should hurry that up. You'll be fifty in about six months? Your eggs are boiling inside you as we speak."

Something gets stuck in my aunt's throat, too. "Seriously, Tommy!"

He nods. "Dead ass, Chrysalis. I tried to keep your secret that you're old as dirt, but it's not fair to your boy toy Derek behind you."

She raises both hands in the air. "We're a year apart! I'm thirty-four! He's thirty-three!"

Derek chuckles and pulls her hands down then wraps them around his back, making her lean into his chest. He should. Aunt Chrys handles grown men for a living as a bounty hunter two cities over in much more fast-paced and crime-infested Spindle.

Uncle Tommy's skinny ass will not stand a chance. He wobbles his head and crosses his hands across his abdomen. "If that's your story, sister, I love you enough to stick to it with you."

Aunt Chrys looks back at Derek. "Can I kill him now?"

Derek gives her a 'let it go, babe' smirk.

Natalia shakes her head behind them, with Luke Jr. wiggling in her arms. So short, she's barely visible in the crowd. "Why do you all take anything out of Tommy's mouth so seriously? He's a clown."

Pops grunts. "It's the shit that comes out of his mouth that ticks us off. He has no filter whatsoever."

"I'll tell you what needs a filter, Frank," Uncle Tommy starts. "*Your* stomach does. At least the women will drop their loads. Yours needs an X painted on it so helicopters can land safely during the freak blizzards that trap people in their homes sometimes."

"Shut up, Tommy," Pops spits then pulls the latch on the glass screen door to get to the brass knob of the oak barrier that's shielding Mama O from my, Malisa's, and the rest of the family's silliness. Pops is doing his damndest to escape Tommy's.

Tommy catches the glass door, following right behind him. "I'm telling you, Frank, you will save a lot of lives if you become a helipad."

The porch empties quickly, when everyone marches single file inside, leaving the inside door open for us.

Halfway to the porch, Astrid's shoulders begin to bounce in front of me, laughing quietly. "Are they always like this?"

"Whenever Unk, which is Uncle Tommy, is around, yes. That's only some of the Owens that you saw. Two of my aunts are probably still decorating in the gardens with Apollo's mother. Almost everyone has kids except Unk, Aunt Chrys who's divorced, and the twins, aunt Jen and

Barbie who work with Aunt Chrys. Unk is the only one that swears he's hilarious though."

"He is," she says just as we reach the bottom step. "I can tell they're good people."

"They are," I say proudly. "But don't let them fool you. They're probably all waiting in the living room for us, and they'll all be nice in front of you. As soon as I show you to the bathroom, the Spanish Inquisition will begin for me. I'm not looking forward to it. They'll catch you alone too, so we can't get our stories straight. Mama O is more cop than we are." That's as much preparation for what's coming as I can give her.

"I'm ready for it."

"What aren't you ready for, Astrid?" It would be perfect if she says raising our child alone.

She stops and looks back. "Loving you, Blake."

Her answer catches me off guard. Will she ever stop surprising the hell out of me? I stumble to a halt, not sure if she loves me or not, or maybe not anymore. Before I can ask her to enlighten me, she climbs the stairs and vanishes inside the house. If she does love me, is it enough to keep her here with me?

"Holy shit! Blake's girl looks just like Malisa up close," Uncle Tommy says from inside the house, where Astrid is alone. "Lydia, you can stop your henpecking now. Blake's finally found what he's been needing to settle down finally."

"What's that, Tommy?" she yells back.

"A copy of Malisa!"

I expected everyone to comment on their similarity, just not that damn loudly. I flinch, charge the front steps as if they're my enemy, and then sling the glass door wide open. It crashes into the wicker loveseat, which skids into the matching rocking chair on the porch. If my uncle's words are sending pure dismay undulating through me, who knows what they're doing to Astrid right now?

I step over the threshold into the living area that is bigger than standard, addressed with white contemporary furniture with brown wood trimming, and filled with family predictably. I feel justified in wanting to shield Astrid from being dubbed an extra for Malisa and keeping her at arms' length to ward off the jokes that would surely come her way. Uncle Tommy is only being flip about her resemblance to Malisa. That's all he ever does about anything. Still, everything inside me recoils on itself. Just about anyone who associates with the Powers are cruel enough to insult Astrid about it behind her back and to her face.

Mercifully, the Owens aren't heartless enough to do that. However, Mama O will take the first chance she gets to get down to the nitty gritty, questioning why I felt the need to keep Astrid undercover, along with what I see in her. That's going to be an awkward conversation to navigate. Who wants to be interrogated by the parental units about anything? If all goes well, it won't last long.

A massive palm swings out from the side and lands in the center of my chest, stopping me in the doorway after it collides with a huge artificial flower arrangement in a Grecian urn sitting beside the door. It tilts over on its side. I sputter when fake petals slap me on the side of my face, then I push the urn to its original upright position with the backside of my hand. I'm not about to chance it finishing falling over and breaking, provoking Natalia's wrath. Everything that can go wrong is going wrong today already, no need for shattered decorations to happen too.

The hand on my chest falls away. Uncle Luke whirls around on me from his place in front of the window, on the other side of the urn. His fury is worse than his wife's. Normally, he's a sedate bull. Right now, I'm poking at it after storming into his house, something I wasn't allowed to do when I was little. Won't stop me from making sure Astrid is alright, though.

"Move, Uncle Luke."

He doesn't. "Slow down, tiger. Astrid's fine." He looks over his shoulder. "Listen to your brother and shut up for real sometimes, Tommy. Damn!"

I'll believe Astrid is okay when I see that for myself, but she's nowhere to be seen, neither is Malisa "Where is Astrid?"

"You better tell him, Luke, before he kicks your ass," Uncle Tommy instigates with a wide smile, from the couch on the other side of the room. "And you won't stand a chance because you're just as old as your sister Chrysalis is, bruh, even if you are the baby of six. You still greeted Jesus when he was born."

Uncle Luke's hand balls into fists at his sides, and twists at the waist, giving Tommy his full attention. "One, kicking my ass in my own house isn't even possible, Tommy. Two, keep talking, and we're going to see if the only muscle on your scrawny body, which is your mouth by the way, can keep me off *your* ass. Three, and this one is for you, Blake." He swivels back around to me. "Don't disrespect my house like that again. Astrid's is in my bathroom with Malisa. It's the only one Malisa will use, and Astrid is welcome to it, too. The walls are very well insulated by the way, and you know we're not going to hurt her, so calm your ass down."

I look him directly in the eyes, intending to do no such thing. "I'm sorry, Uncle Luke, and I know you all won't hurt her physically. There's other ways to hurt someone unintentionally though." With words or lack thereof, and I should know.

Uncle Luke cocks his head, clearly confused.

Uncle Tommy tilts his too. His mouth lifts in one corner. "Still didn't get that porridge yet, huh, Luke?"

Mama O walks into the room from the far left corner that's connected to the kitchen, calmly wiping her hands on a dish towel. "What's really got you rushing up in here like you have no home training, son? And I know you have some, because I taught it to you."

Let the 'getting down to the nitty gritty' begin.

Her imposing presence shuts down most of the aggression in me, always has out of respect. I start to rub the back of my neck, where a ridiculous amount of tension has gathered. "I didn't tell Astrid exactly how much she looks like Malisa, and I don't want people saying nasty things about it to her or behind her back because of it."

Uncle Luke puts his backside to the window again, to observe. He's like Pops in that regard; they speak only when they have something to say.

Uncle Tommy's eyes lose their normal liveliness and deviousness, to fill with remorse. "I didn't mean to say anything that'll hurt her, Blake. Just calling it like I see it, like I usually do. She wasn't even in the room if that's what got your panties in your crack."

"Unk, I heard you all the way outside. She probably heard you too."

He stands up. "Okay, let's get serious for a minute." That's something he tries his hardest not to ever do, and it takes me by surprise.

"Somebody take a damn picture of this because it isn't going to last long," Aunt Chrys snipes from beside Derek on the loveseat pressed against the far wall.

Uncle Tommy shushes her. "Blake, you're not so much as worried about Astrid hearing me as you are about her finding out that you had a crush on Malisa as a child, and if she'll wonder if she's just a fill-in."

"She's not a fill-in, Unk. Never was, and I don't want her to ever think that."

Why the hell didn't I say that to her before someone mentioned it?

Because I'm a coward, afraid she'll feel exactly how Uncle Tommy called it, a fill-in for Malisa. We would have surely gone downhill from there until I lost her. I did anyway, for a totally different reason.

"I don't think she is either, but Blake, we all know this goes much deeper than what Astrid will think. Someone somewhere, not me of course, has developed a feeling or had a tickle in the crotch for someone they shouldn't have. Hell, some families even encourage inbreeding, but you and Malisa don't qualify, so there is nothing bad about any feeling you had as a teen for her. You didn't act on it, and that makes you a better man than most adults. She wouldn't have done too bad with you as her first boyfriend, but we didn't think she'd let you sow your oats in her fields anyway. You two depended on each other to be there for one another too much to risk ruining your relationship over sex."

"She's still too young at twenty-six for being sown *and* plowed if you ask me," Pops grumbles.

Uncle Tommy waves him off. "That point is moot, Frank. She's been incubating Apollo's super rockets for eight months, remember? Listen, Blake. Your little puppy love lasted all of two minutes before *you* decided for yourself that Malisa was off limits. Only a good boy growing into a good man would've done that, when young boys and some old men who know better still plow through everything in a skirt, if they can. But it doesn't matter how well the Owens raised you or how much you hold us in your heart, technically, Malisa is never really off limits to you. Well, she is now of course because she found the good man for her. Just don't develop a crush on me, looking for the next best Owens. I'm telling you up front that I don't like you like that."

I chuckle, like he intended for me to, a lot less angry with him just like he wants me to be.

"And Tommy's a clown again," Aunt Chrys mumbles.

59

He looks back at her, frowning. "For Pete's sake, be quiet, Chrysalis. I got a little more seriousness left in me and I need to get it out. I'm feeling heavy and icky and shit. Back to you, Blake. If Astrid can't understand any of that or that coincidence is a bitch sometimes, maybe she's not the girl for you after all, but you've got to stop punishing yourself for recognizing the perfect, flawed example of what you should want in a woman. And you're making too big a damn deal out of your woman looking like your sister. They're called doppelgangers. Nothing you or anyone else can do about perfect copies of other people showing up in other families or your heart picking one to love. You definitely love something about her if she's incubating *your* super rocket and you ran up in your Uncle Luke's house with your chest puffed out… or you're feeling suicidal. Whatever the case is, just don't call her by the wrong name, or she'll gang up on your ass with whatever weapons she can get her hands on and doppel your nuts. True story, nephew!"

Derek falls over behind Aunt Chrys, who covers her mouth with both hands. Her eyes begin to water. I browse the room, taking in the nonjudgmental gazes belonging to my family. Most are too busy laughing their asses off to be judgmental about anything. They truly understand more than I ever thought they would about the guilt that's ridden for me for so long. Maybe Astrid will be understanding, too.

"You *all* knew when I thought I'd hid my attraction to Malisa?" And I hadn't lost them at all, or it would've happen long ago.

Mama O smiles and begins to fold the towel neatly, while nodding. "Everyone knew *but* Malisa, Blake. That's how small your crush was at a time, when kids can't make up their minds about *who* they like, including you. I'm pretty sure if you wanted her that badly, you'd have told her. Instead, you've been feeling ashamed about your body turning on you, but you've always liked the good girls and have always been more overprotective as hell of Malisa than anything, annoyingly so sometimes. It's not your fault that you had the perfect way to give Apollo hell about hurting her either… I *might* have used that to my benefit, as well." After admitting that, grudgingly, she sits down on Pops' knee. "You and I know that competition makes a real man straighten up. We tested Apollo in our own way, like most families would, and he passed. Most brothers couldn't express interest in their sister just to make a man see what he has like you did. Anyone that wants someone for themselves doesn't stick around to decorate a wedding venue so they can marry someone else, and make sure they get a happily ever after. Does that sound a like a man who still has a crush on someone? If it does to Astrid, you send her to me."

Not with Mama O's penchant for violence.

"No, but thank you," I say quickly. This was practice for when I'm facing my father. "This conversation is weird enough."

She points at me. "You're right about that. Since it's already weird, I might as well ask the question that you knew I would. Why do you like Astrid so much? You've already covered why you hid her from us."

"I'm sorry about that, Mama O. I should've known you all would understand. The answer to why I like her so much is simple. My heart chose her before I knew anything about her. Her independent streak is adorable. She's always smiling, and never asked me for anything despite who my parents are, not even my heart, but it's hers. If I had gotten a say in who took my breath away at first sight, I'd have spared Astrid from ever being put in this position. If I have my way, I'll be good man to her, and if it makes everyone feel any better, I haven't met her parents either."

Apollo, who's grinning wide beside Pops, points to his chest. "Tried and true good man over here who knows his woman's people. And she knows mine." He holds up a single finger. "All one of them." Sienna, his mother, is all that's left of his family from Canada.

Pops turns his head and frowns in his face. "Really? You're going to gloat right now, Apollo?"

He nods his head vigorously. "Damn straight, Frank, soon-to-be-father-in-law!"

I snicker at my future brother-in-law's smug gesture, feeling for the first time, in a long time, a little less weighed down with guilt over things I truly couldn't control. "Malisa knows about the crush because I told her, but I thought if you all knew, I'd—"

"Upset us, and then we'd push you out the family," Pops interrupts. "You haven't disappointed anyone, son. It's almost impossible for you to do that, and I think your biggest fear is losing us for one reason or another. That's heartwarming and this'll be the only time I say that word, but real family loves each other through it all, or Tommy would've been out on his ass after his first joke. Hell, he's half a joke away from being pushed out now, but you're not."

Uncle Tommy's head dips down in Pops' direction. "Half a joke away from being pushed out, huh, Frank? You're going to pay for that. I got more jokes than you got stomach, brother. Remember that."

I chuckle despite the heaviness still on my conscious about Astrid. There are things she still needs to know about me. "Losing the Owens is *one* of my biggest fears, Pops."

He nods, in his all-knowing way. "Losing Astrid is the other. How long have you been in love with her?"

I scrub my hair backwards on the top of my head and blow out my mouth. "From the damn moment I laid eyes on her two years ago."

"Then you go through the fire with her, son, by sitting her down and talking to her about everything that concerns you. If she comes out the other side with you, she's a keeper, but you need to talk to her pronto. Let her know what she's up against in your world, like your snobby biological parents who are still trying to get you to take over their businesses. And while you're stalling about giving them an answer, because you don't want to just say no to them though you see right through their manipulating, you should probably mention to Astrid that they barely tolerate anyone who isn't a Powers or wealthy in their own right."

"I planned to talk to her about all of that, after it was all over. But what if talking to her now about it is the worst thing for her condition? Pregnant women are affected by everything. The last thing I want to do is jeopardize my family's health because of my burdens."

"You're still stalling, Blake, but you'd be surprised at how much a woman can go through when pregnant. If she hears about any of this from anyone but you, like Tommy's big mouth for instance, you may lose her anyway. And your baby will go where she goes."

I swipe my hand down my face, and acknowledge that I haven't hidden anything from anyone but Astrid. "Damn, what don't you know, Pops?"

He smiles just as arrogantly as Apollo is doing. "Blake, you're more overprotective than Lydia is, which is why you're in this mess. But thanks to Lydia, there's not much I don't know about my kids. In other words, my wife is nosy as hell and still talks to your mother, but you hid Astrid well from all of us. I'm going to need some lessons on how to do that. I can't even hide my weight gain from Lydia. She be all up *in* my business."

The room erupts with laughter.

Mama O glimpses back at her husband with a small smile on her face. "Oh Frank, you're going to pay for that too. Tommy's jokes are going to seem like child's play compared to how I can make you suffer. Remember that."

Pops' smile evaporates. "See what you've gotten me into, Blake?"

Malisa walks through the doorway in the right corner of the room, with a good grip on the wall to stabilize the load in front of her and a lopsided grin on her face. "Blake, if it makes you feel any better, you're not the only one that's passed me up for someone else that looks like me after two minutes. Derek decided that Aunt Chrys is the better woman for him, remember, after coming all the way out here to eat breakfast with me? You don't see them worrying themselves to death about it, and they shouldn't. She *is* the better woman for him. Sometimes, how we get to the one we're meant to be with isn't the straightforward path we'd like to travel. It wasn't like that for Apollo and me either, but you don't have to make the crooks and turns harder to travel than they already are either by worrying about every little bitty thing that could go wrong along the way. You're missing out on the fun during the journey."

Then Astrid manifests beside Malisa. How much has she heard?

Chapter Five

Blake

The air stiffens then turns stifling. Is it too much to ask that I get to break just one thing about my life down to Astrid slowly? She strolls toward me, with a blank expression on her face, stopping when her exhales are fanning my neck. She's still too far away, after being gone for one hundred and eighty-one days.

"You can stop looking at me like you've seen a ghost, Blake. I heard just about everything said in here. As you can see, I'm fine and still pregnant. It doesn't take me that long to use the bathroom, or for women to gossip."

I shift my weight to one foot, hoping life is now through with overriding my decisions of when she needs to find out something about me. Tonight is not that damn far away. "Well, I'm *not* fine, Astrid. I'll do anything to not lose you and my son, again."

She rubs her hands together between us. "So I see you'll do anything, including keeping me in the dark a little longer about what else troubles you, huh?"

"It isn't so much as keeping you in the dark, love. Tonight—"

"Yes, it is," Uncle Tommy cuts me off.

Pops' hand slaps the arm of the sofa. "Shut up, Tommy!"

Again, I massage the backside of my neck, where the tension is getting tighter. "I'm only protecting you the best way I know how, Astrid. I'd planned—"

"Your idea of protecting is leaving me out in the cold, Blake, unprepared for what *we* can't control. What other people say is one of those things." She huffs air. "But I have it on good authority that your parents didn't give you good examples of what it means to fully trust someone with what's going on in that head of yours, after abandoning you emotionally. You're not a kid anymore though. You chose to not trust me to stick beside you no matter what comes our way, like being a dead ringer for Malisa. I also know that if it wasn't for the Owens, you'd be a troublemaker instead of full of troubles that make you embrace everyone with one hand and push them away with the other. I should've learned about the innocent crush and your broken upbringing from you *before* you decided to treat me like your girl but wouldn't call me that. Well, I didn't learn all that from you, and *that* is what's hurting me right now… I can't trust you, Blake."

A haze of defeat descends upon me. Pops' advice has come too little too late; she's already heard secondhand what should've come from the horse's mouth. Now, there's a new break in our relationship to repair; make Astrid trust me again, starting now.

"Astrid, I know I never deserved your trust in the first place, but have faith that this won't ever happen again. I'll talk your damn ears off if that's what it takes to get you back with me. I've learned to not let the best thing slip through my fingers, and it was wrong to keep you disconnected from my real life. All I wanted to do was keep you happy, and I didn't think I could do that if you were tangled up in the shit that surrounds me every day, all day. I won't ever be able to say I'm sorry enough for that. I do need you to believe from this point forward you've had my heart from day one and whatever troubles I have you'll hear from me first."

She looks over my shoulder, or tries to—it's not possible when she's only five foot two. "Well, if it sets your mind at ease, it's cool having a look-a-like who's sweet as Malisa. I admit it was a little startling when she answered the door, but I'm used to it already, and I can handle whatever opinion someone throws my way about it. That's not a problem for us anymore at least." One problem down. Only God knows how many more to go. Progress, if I look at it from the 'cup is half-full' angle.

"I know you will handle it, Astrid. I've never known you to lose your head about anything, and I should've trusted you to be you. I won't make that mistake again. So, where do we go from here? Hopefully to the truck for some privacy. There's none to be had in here."

A flash of amusement crosses her face, then her manner switches right back to subdued. I'll give up everything to bring her infectious joy and lively spirit back, and mend whatever I've broken inside her.

"I did lose my head, Blake, when I panicked and ran home to my parents. I know I shouldn't have done that, well, at least not before telling—"

I drop one finger across her lips. "You should've went to wherever you felt the safest and most taken care of. Our baby and you deserve that, and I'm not mad about finding out about him eight months too late. I'm just glad I didn't miss every milestone in your pregnancy."

"Six months too late," she forces around my finger. I move it so she can speak freely. "I went to the doctor, when I thought I'd come down with the flu. I was already eight weeks gone."

"I wish you had told me were sick, Astrid. I'd have gone with you. You wouldn't have gone through any of this alone. I'm so sorry that you didn't think my love extended to going through thick and thin with you."

She swallows deeply. "I wasn't alone. I had my parents. I don't know how I'm going to take your parents though. I don't have a blue blood background, nor would I trade my family for one."

Besides the initial shock that I gave her when I first confessed my love for her, she's starting to tune me out every time I mention my feelings now. My parents are fast becoming the least of my problems. My worst decision, letting Astrid leave without giving her my whole heart, is coming back to bite me in the ass the hardest.

"Don't worry about the Powers, Astrid. I'll handle them when it comes to you. I just need to know are we staying here or in Harrison?"

When I think about it, Harrison may just be the best solution, which makes it harder for my parents to interfere and show up out of the blue. And they will.

"Harrison in Utah!" Malisa yelps. She may be the only one besides Astrid familiar with the cities in that state. She still works there as Apollo's vice president, when she's not traveling back and forth between there and here, checking on her new home.

Apollo puts his finger to his mouth. "Shhh, baby. Let them talk."

"But, Apollo," she whispers loudly. "I need someone who can empathize with what I'm going through while pregnant, and I can call her sister. She's the closest that I'm going to get to having one. Blake was and is a *horrible* excuse for a sibling. He doesn't talk to me about anything anymore."

Uncle Tommy's laughter blasts off. "Malisa, no one can empathize with you. Who in here has ever had a whole playground around their waist? Not even your father can brag about that."

Astrid's chest bounces with her amusement. Every time the conversation dips below uncomplicated and fun, her tinkling laugh dries up. I rather keep the smile on her face.

"This is what I go through in Arrow, Astrid. It doesn't matter *where* we stay. Malisa has all kinds of ways at her disposal to travel, to see you and the baby. Save me and *please* take me to Harrison." She giggles, and I've successfully concealed my desperation to be wherever she is.

Her fingers stretch through the space between us toward mine, finally reaching for me on her own. When she's linked to me, she looks deeply into my eyes. "Blake, you can't move to Harrison. You have a job here that you love, and we still have so much to talk about before we make any decisions regarding our child's future. You must make one concerning your parents first. I'm not going to build any kind of relationship with you just to have them tear it down. Something should be done about your habit for withholding information. Giving me all your body is one thing. Letting

70

someone into your world is something else entirely, and I don't know if it's that easy for you to just change overnight." Her uncertainty in me gives me hope for us and, finally, something to build on. It's not her trust, that's for sure, as much as I'd like for it to be, but her willingness to give me a chance is as good as any for a starting place.

"You and now the baby are my world, Astrid. Give me this month to prove it."

She drops her head, starts fiddling with my fingers. "If you don't?" The doubts ripple off her like waves.

I release her hands to lift her chin up with my thumbs. "Then I'll move to Harrison, help you raise our child, and never bother you about loving you again." But losing her again is not an option.

"Okay," she whispers.

"Okay." Crisis averted, I decide to drop the conversation. There's just too many damn people in here ear-hustling.

Malisa takes two steps inside the room then sinks into an armchair with a throne back. "Oh thank you, Jesus. Now what else needs to be done for the wedding and reception? I'll take Blake's spot in helping since he needs to spend time with Astrid and secure her in the family for me. Uh, I meant for him."

Apollo gets to his feet from the chair sitting catty-corner to Malisa's, and steps into the aisle between them that Malisa and Astrid used to reenter the room, getting ready to put his foot down. "Nuh huh, my Lisa. I'm worried as hell about your blood pressure. It goes up whenever you stand up. The only standing you should be doing is when we say I do, and you know I'm right."

She sighs. "You're right, Apollo, but where's the helium tank and balloons you were supposed to bring to me while I was sitting?"

He groans. The rest of their discussion gets lost when Astrid's mouth becomes all I can see. It's impossible to look at it and not want it molded to mine. I move in for a stolen kiss, but the softness of her lips is enough to steal my right mind. The room shrinks to just her and me. I stand rigid, afraid to move, with my mouth pressed to hers, wanting more but satisfied with what I can get until she chooses to disrupt the fragile connection.

A soft moan emanates from her. Her tongue pushes at the slit in my lips that open, allowing her inside immediately. I let her set the pace, whether our tongues will battle or dance together. She chooses to tango, slowly, until my jeans are a prison for my erection again, her essence coating my insides. Chests rising and falling fast, soundless music dies an unhurried death as the kiss winds down so we both can surface for air.

"Shit, Blake, we weren't supposed to do that again," she whispers, while staring up at me with the windows of her soul unguarded.

Distance is what she wants. Proximity and the pull of her attraction is keeping her orbiting too closely to me. She's not happy about it.

I mesh our foreheads together and weld my palms to hers. "Well, I was going for a quick 'seal the deal of you staying for the month' peck. You started the mouth wrangling."

Raised voices emit from Uncle Luke's den, snagging both of our attention. The living area is completely empty, oddly. It's still not settled who is going to take over my duties. Astrid giggles at the amount of conversations that's taking place in one room simultaneously.

"They're going to kill each other if you don't help. We'll have the reception to talk… I think."

I laugh. "Yes, they can hover like helicopters, and they're going to kill each other anyway, but they recognize and respect crucial moments when a couple needs to be left alone too. No one will mind if I spend time with you. That's what I really want to do, and there's only a few more things that need to be done for the wedding. They should be able to handle it."

She smirks. "I wouldn't want to take you away from your family on Malisa's special day, and I really don't have anything to wear to a wedding or reception. This casual dress and flip flops make it seem like I popped up at the last minute and got an invitation for the occasion. Well, I did, but—"

"Oh no ma'am," Malisa says from the doorway of the den that she's suddenly standing sideways in, hovering. "I got you covered, Astrid. My cream romper for the reception should fit you just fine, but stop feeling like you're underdressed. My wedding dress is made on the same style as the one you're wearing, and it's comfortable enough for me to wear until I get to the hotel. Whoever doesn't like either dress can go to you know where, and I'll be in flats the whole time. No fancy shoes for me either, but I'm going to warn you that you better talk to Blake while you can afterwards because he's not going to make it to tomorrow. He's kept the best thing that ever happened to him from me."

"Well, I knew someone wasn't going to make it," I grumble, officially a dead man standing who'd predicted his own demise without knowing it.

Apollo appears behind Malisa, smiling. "Blake, I wasn't going to have one, but would you like to be my best man today? It looks like you're going to need practice standing in front of a preacher and you already have the outfit."

Astrid shifts her weight from one foot to the other, as if she's quietly panicking that I might drop down on one knee any minute now. A proposal will leave my mouth at some point, but not yet. It's her that's not ready for me now, and there is no rush for her to be. I squeeze her fingers, hoping I'm reassuring her that everything will work at the speed that *she* wants our lives to go for here on out.

Malisa claps her hands happily and lands a smack of her lips under Apollo's chin, again. I look down at Astrid, who nods her approval. If I thought for one minute she'd feel uncomfortable sitting by herself with guests she doesn't know, I wouldn't say yes to Apollo, but she's mostly fearless when it comes to the unknown. Hasn't met one person that she can't make love her. Apollo, on the other hand, has astonished the hell out of me with his request. We didn't get off on the right foot when he followed Malisa home at the beginning of this year. He has proven himself though, and I'll be glad to stand beside him.

"I'd be honored to be your best man, Apollo, but I don't have a speech prepared." Their wedding is supposed to be a humble family and close friends' affair without the extra hoopla, which doesn't explain why the immediate family is required to wear formal gear.

If I was as smart as I think I am, I'd have asked why I was being fitted for a suit a week after he proposed.

Apollo walks over and whacks me on the back. "You can wing it."

Astrid shakes her head. "You don't want him to do that. There's no telling what he's going to say, with lots of f-bombs and other four letter words in his speech." It's the truth.

Apollo glances back at Malisa, who has a stricken look on his face. Her head swivels around to Mama O, who's perching on the edge of Uncle Luke's recliner in his man-cave. She rubs the bottom side of her chin and transfers her gaze to Pops, who's sitting in the chair. He looks down at his hands, examining his nails.

Apollo's wide-eyes return to me. "Okay, I'll give the best man speech at the reception then. You can help finish putting up the equipment as a substitute."

My mouth falls open as I pretend to be shocked at his decision. "I've never felt so dissed. It's because I'm white and adopted, isn't it?"

"The truth is supposed to set you free, Blake," ejects out of Malisa's smiling lips as she waddles over, to lean against Apollo.

I shake my head then grin. "Yes, it does, Lisa Poo… right after it stabs you through the heart."

75

However, I'm completely fine with not having to come up with pretty words on the fly that are supposed to be sentimental enough to make people sob. Well, someone would, but it'll be from embarrassment. Curse words will surely fly out my mouth as soon as I breach the two-drink limit.

****

A few hours later

A curving runner of red carpet leads up to the designated place for Malisa's and Apollo's vows. An enormous pointed Roman arch, with attached curved extensions that's needs four widely-spaced colonnades to rest on, stands over my head and Apollo's, along with the preacher's. He's separated from us by a short banister created from fat, stubby posts. Each piece of the arch-system is extremely heavy, and a bitch to set in place. Especially when I must contend with six different female opinions from my aunts, Mama O, and the wedding planner—everyone had a different way they wanted everything placed.

It's not shocking that I got stuck dealing with all of them, climbing a ladder, and the heavy-lifting when the men with their feet planted firmly on the ground needed to position the columns that holds up the arch correctly. Who gets the most hazardous duty of equipment erection is decided by Mama O and Pops, and whether Apollo will bust his ass falling on his wedding day or not. My bones being the youngest and potentially healing faster than everyone else's is included in the deciding factor as well.

As far as I'm concerned, I'd place everything single-handedly if it gets this wedding started that much faster. Fortunately, the only thing left to do at this point is wait for Malisa to walk down the aisle. I'm already tired of only being able to stare at Astrid. I wouldn't have gotten the opportunity to do that if I'd lost the argument between Malisa and I, which took place through Uncle Luke's bedroom door. While they were getting dressed, Malisa made her demands for Astrid to sit on the bride's side of course, but I want Astrid where I can see her.

To get my way, all I had to do was start complaining about being white and adopted. When I vowed that I wasn't letting Astrid out of my sight until she knew how I felt about her, I meant it. That includes not letting her out of my sight until she feels the same way I do too, if I can help it. Too bad I can't use the same complaint of my race and rank in the Owens clan to get her to love me back.

One side of her lips coated in more gloss, which I plan to kiss right back off again, lift in an edgy, crooked smile as she knots her fingers tightly in her lap. Subtle hints of tension. I'd go to her and soothe whatever's worrying her, but a soft breeze carries the sound of the golf cart's quiet engine around the shrubbery beside Astrid. Pops got the cushy responsibility of driving Malisa to the far end of the carpet, which she'll follow to her new beginning with Apollo.

Finally, the show is about to begin.

Then I inhale two nostrils full of pollen, sneeze, and give a nasty look to the bushes that are concealing Malisa from her guests. Astrid and Apollo's mother, Sienna, put their heads together and snicker quietly at my expense. Sienna seems to be the only woman here that's laidback. I guess she would have to learn to be, to survive losing Apollo to the shady childcare system in his birth city. His father would die before they could find their only child who'll be a successful businessman, when information of his only living relative finds the light of day.

The Wedding March begins to play, thank God. I sneeze again and have visions of chopping down the damn shrubbery when Natalia's and Uncle Luke's backs are turned. Astrid laughs a little louder, probably reading my mind. Maybe I should leave the bushes alone. If my allergies make her feel comfortable enough to keep her from bolting down the aisle like she's a runaway bride, I'll sneeze all day.

Malisa and Pops finally emerge on the runner, arm in arm. I huff with relief. Apollo breathes in deeply then touches the corner of his eye.

Oh my God, he's going to cry!

I didn't sign up for comforting a grown ass man sobbing while filling in as his best man. Still, I reach up and pat his back awkwardly. I think that's what a best man is supposed to do. If it isn't, Apollo is screwed. I don't have expertise in this area, and at this point, I don't want any. I have enough problems just dealing with my own emotions.

Malisa grins wide enough at her husband-to-be for anyone to see her smile a mile away. Really, it's only thirty yards away, so I'm practically blinded by her happiness. What would it take to get Astrid to smile at me like that? Apollo distracts me from my thoughts when he rushes forward, to reach Malisa before she can turn the corner and parade down the aisle.

"Man, what are you doing?" I yell after him.

No wedding that I've ever attended required the groom to meet the bride, cancelling out some of her time to shine. Apollo doesn't even look back. I think he only sees Malisa and their unborn children.

Definitely can't miss the babies.

He offers her his arm. She shoves her bouquet through the space between his bent elbow and body. The guests and I stand and watch them take their precious time getting back to the starting point for Apollo, who's eyeballing Malisa instead of watching where he's going. Since she's staring at him too, I'm pretty sure Pops is walking… it's more like he's guiding them both down the aisle.

If Apollo's plan is to get her to the alter quicker, it fails epically. Maria, the wedding planner who's dressed in yellow and stilettos that aren't made for outdoors, hangs back behind the last row on the bride's side, shaking her head, which probably hurts. The bottle-blond topknot looks like it's painful and has her gray eyes stretched back to her ears.

Yep, she's definitely irritated.

The teardrop diamonds in Malisa's ears swinging ten times for every one step she takes isn't helping the planner's disposition—Malisa's march was way faster in rehearsal. Enough minutes pass for me to make a long mental list of things I need to buy before my son's birth. The wedding planner checks her watch twice, which incites me to eyeball mine and decide something monumental. Unless Astrid demands it, I'm not having an actual wedding ceremony with all the trimmings. There's every chance that I'll lose my composure and rush her on the aisle, too. I'd rather not embarrass myself like that. Although, I doubt if Apollo feels an ounce of shame. Neither would I.

When Apollo, Malisa, and Pops are standing beside me, still linked arm in arm, Pops waits for the preacher to ask who gives the woman away. Then he answers, kisses Malisa's cheek, and takes his seat beside Mama O. Immediately, she leans over into Pops' chest and starts to weep loudly. More sniveling arises from the guests. Pops pulls his wife closer with his arm draped around her back, then pats his eyes with the lilac handkerchief from his breast pocket.

Yep, no ceremony for me.

Dry-eyed Malisa, who's probably the only one composed besides me, turns and waves Astrid over. Astrid's eyes bounce around the crowd, with an apprehensive yet hopeful expression that Malisa isn't beckoning *her* out of all the guests. Her luck doesn't run that well though; Malisa gives up on waving to her and calls her name instead. Astrid's eyes round out like saucers before I step forward, to help her out of her chair. At least, I won't be embarrassed by myself at the next thing the bride and groom do that isn't rehearsed.

After hustling Astrid to her impromptu bridesmaid's position beside Malisa, Apollo prompts the preacher to begin. The next thing I know, Apollo's head is dipping, and he and Malisa are kissing. I didn't hear them recite their vows, too busy taking note of every curve that becomes visible in the satin, sleeveless fabric that Astrid is wearing whenever the wind blows. The sporadic gentle draft takes advantage of the material loose enough to play with, making it hard to keep my levelheadness. Another of part of me is hard too. It stiffens even more every time a gust shapes Astrid's clothes to the swell of her fuller breasts, rounder hips, and stomach over and over.

I'm not sure if most men get turned on by the sight of their child distending from their woman's body, but I've just learned that I sure as hell do. The penguin suit doubles as a haven for heat. A sheen of sweat pops out on my brow. I mop it with one hand, pull on my collar with the other. A trickle of perspiration runs down my spine. I get testy.

"It's hot in this fucking thing," I grumble under my breath. Haven't passed the two-drink anything and I'm already cursing. Oh yeah, the best man speech is better off weighing down someone else's shoulders.

Malisa giggles against Apollo's mouth, butchering their first kiss as husband and wife.

"That's why we warned you, Apollo, that you didn't want him to speak," she says between chuckles.

Apollo lifts his head and shakes it. Uncle Tommy snorts from the second row on the bride's side. The preacher gives me the evil eye and slams his bible shut. I realize I didn't do a good job of keeping my misery to myself.

"Sorry," I murmur, and then squint at Astrid, who's cupping her hand over her mouth, but her mirth is escaping anyway.

Now, how fair is that it that she's laughing when I'm suffering from overheating… and dying to be inside her.

"You're going to pay for this, Astrid," I warn.

"*What?*" she shrieks. "I didn't do anything!" Then more laughter erupts from her.

"No, your parents did it. If you weren't so damn beautiful, I wouldn't be this damn hot," I snarl.

The priest groans. The first three rows of guests on each side of the lane laugh.

"We know who's getting married next," someone yells from the back row on the bride's side.

Suddenly, everyone knows that Astrid is my girl, or rather that I want her to be, and I didn't have to say a word. Well, not while face to face with anyone anyway, but I knew just being near her would broadcast my feelings for her. Hell, I'd shout it to the world if I thought she wouldn't mind, but she does. I clench my teeth together, and just stare at... well, you know who I'm looking at. Everybody does at this point.

The signature sizzling look of hers covers her caramel features before it flits away. Astrid seems be having difficulty with keeping her emotions on lockdown. Good. More warmness forces itself under my clothes. My erection slams against my zipper.

On impact, I grunt and tap Apollo on the shoulder. "When do we get to change back into streetwear?" Everything that we practiced in rehearsal has skipped right out of my head.

Apollo chuckles, turns around, and whispers, "You can go now, Blake. I wouldn't want you attacking Astrid in front of everyone, but be on the other side of the wall in twenty minutes for the reception or you'll have to answer for why you're not there to our family by yourself."

"That sounds like a good idea to me, and I'm not going to attack her," I growl, at Astrid. 'Attacking her' should be done only while we're sequestered, if I can get her to agree to it and in a room by ourselves.

She winks at me with the eye only the preacher can see. "I'll go too. I have to use the bathroom."

The preacher's mouth falls open, along with mine. Poor man, he's learning the hard way how bold Astrid can really be sometimes, just to get a laugh out of someone or her point across. You must be daring to show up at someone else's house and announce to whoever answers the door that you're pregnant by the yet-to-be-best man.

"You know that you have to chaperone her down the aisle right, Blake?" Malisa asks, with a mischievous grin on her face.

We didn't practice that last night either, but we should have.

"Fine, let's go, Astrid." I respond hurriedly, then get close enough to her to smell the jasmine fragrance that wrecks my senses and mind instantly, every time.

This is going to be one long ass stroll.

Chapter Six

Blake

When I offer her my arm, I hold my breath. I don't know why I'm doing that either. She wraps her hand arm my bicep, with a huge smile on her face. The inability to breathe goes away. Instinctively, my right foot takes off. I forget to watch where I'm going. The woman at my side is much more interesting. Luckily, I can walk a straight line while sober, or there's no telling who all I'd have run over in their chairs.

Astrid isn't making things any safer for the guests; she's not looking where she's going either. Three strides later, I forget everything and everyone around me except her whiskey-colored eyes, until I walk off the carpet. I'm supposed to follow the bend in it veering to the left, which stops at three golf carts lined up at the end.

When I stop, Astrid sinks an inch. I look down, just to see how far off course onto the lawn I've escorted her. The bottom of her flat, strappy sandals on loan from Malisa have completely vanished into the thick grass. Tiny diamonds arranged across her instep and rose-colored painted toenails reflect pinpoints of sunlight in my eyes. If Apollo was anywhere near Malisa when she bought them, then there are real diamonds on Astrid's feet. It's his plan to give Malisa the world, and he tries at every turn. Sounds like a master plan to me.

"I can walk back to the house, Blake," Astrid whispers, drawing my attention to her mouth. "And I should for the exercise."

"You don't have to, love."

"I do. I want to go back to work soon, and keeping in shape makes sure I heal faster from giving birth… and we can talk on the way to the house."

We do have more of my stupid mistakes to discuss, but I haven't forgotten about her needs. The house isn't a skip and a hop away. "But you have to use the bathroom."

"No, I don't."

"You lied?" I ask, confused. I shouldn't be. Astrid is even more inventive than me when it comes to getting her way, or maybe I just don't put up a big fight because giving her what she wants usually gets me what I want.

So why didn't she ever ask me for my heart? Because she's a smart lady who knew I wasn't ready to give it over to her of my own volition yet. She just didn't know that she'd stolen it from me already.

She grins. "Yep. I didn't drink anything so I wouldn't have to go in the middle of Malisa's and Apollo's nuptials."

I want to believe that she wants to be alone with me for the same reasons I have, and I've never wanted to talk to someone so much in life. I freely admit that I'm desperate to talk to her some more, and for other things to happen. Hopefully, so is she. To keep from bogging her down with my yearnings, just in case they don't match hers, I stick with keeping things light.

"Bad girl, Astrid."

"And I love a bad boy, so sue me." Then she winks again.

I try hard to not add more value to her words than she means to imply. It's easy to want to sleep with someone while not wanting to be with them. I lived like that for the first twenty-four years of my life on purpose. Even if that's how Astrid feels right now, I'll be the bad boy she loves any day, in any way, as long as it's me she wants, until she can't live without me. When her natural sultriness starts to glow a little brighter in her face again, I know what's going to happen as soon as we're alone. Astrid is going to attack me.

Hell yes!

I reach up and take her chin in my fingertips. "Oh love, suing you is the last thing I'm going to do."

"Good."

"Then let's go." I walk forward again, but it hurts the massive wood in my pants to move without plunging into her first. Well, it's going to learn some patience around her if I have to… How in the hell do you teach an erection to calm down?

Stop thinking about it may help, some anyway.

"So you're going back to work?" I ask, determined to drag my mind elsewhere.

Secretly, I hope she doesn't go back to work soon or in Harrison. Nothing is set in stone between us yet, so there is every chance that she'll choose her hometown over me. I have every reason to believe that she wouldn't if I had dealt with my issues first. No matter my good intentions for not doing it, my long list of faults grows by one more. I'd kill to be able to erase just one where it concerns Astrid, and I know which one I'd murder first; the pestering about becoming a true Powers. It'll die a quick death, too.

When that's out the way, I'm informing my parents that I have every intention of marrying Astrid, once she feels safe enough in my love and commitment to her and our growing family. Ashley and Martin are going to take my newest future plans much harder than the last ones that led me to my career. Maybe they'll even disown me. That's probably the best thing they'll ever do for me and Astrid, since they don't believe in diluting the Powers' bloodline with anyone who is less than what they believe is Italian royalty.

Astrid certainly doesn't fit that category, not when she's black and from Small Town, USA with no old money behind her family name. She doesn't have new money either, but she's royalty to me. When I can set up an introduction with my parents to meet my queen, they'll know what she means to me too. I will not be giving her every reason to walk away, *again*.

When she looks away from me, which is never good, I get out of my thoughts of her to concentrate solely on her with my eyes.

"I have to support our child, Blake." She's unquestionably insecure in my love for her.

I cup her chin in my fingers again, and turn her eyes to mine, while we make good time covering the distance between the house and the gardens. "I'll support you both if you want to be a stay-at-home mom for a while, Astrid. I'll support you if you don't. I'll support you if you're mine outright… and I'll support if you aren't."

Do I want to give her the choice of being mine or not? I don't even have to answer that question, do I? But I definitely have to give her room to come around to my way of thinking because if I don't, she'll probably run again.

She swallows deeply, as we approach the glass French doors with tea-light trimming on the outside that leads into what was Natalia's kitchen, now Mama O's. She wouldn't let anyone else cook anything besides the cake for the reception. Astrid's eyes become misty.

Damn. If it isn't one person crying around me, it's another.

I just hope that she's happy enough to cry about my 'best man for her' speech.

"Tell me what's on your mind, sweetheart," I demand softly while I slide the doors open with my empty hand.

Scents from the buffet waiting to be hauled out to the reception area by the wedding planner's minions bomb rush me. My stomach growls, seems like I'm always hungry.

"You're on my mind, Blake… as always," she confesses, softly, reluctantly.

"Is that good or bad?" I'm not stupid enough to deny that either could be the case right now after all the shit I put her through.

"Both," she says simply.

That one word is enough to make my chest tighten up. Suddenly, I have no appetite. We walk between the cabinets that cover the back wall and the covered steam pans that are lined up in front of the casual four-chair dining table, sitting pretty on their stand-up racks, ready to be transported by golf cart to the gardens. I should be dipping into at least one with my fingers, sampling the food while there's no one around to catch me doing it. Instead, I'm watching for the slightest emotional change in Astrid's face. It's all I can bring myself to care about right now.

"Can you explain what 'both' means for me?" Maybe I can ease her mind about some of her issues concerning me before we find the outfits that we changed out of.

We wouldn't be putting them back on anytime soon if we were anywhere but here. My family isn't going to let us miss the reception and wishing Malisa and Apollo well before they take their leave to the one of the Powers' ski resorts located in Aspen. It's my gift to them, registered under Mr. and Mrs. Ford, so my parents don't show up unannounced, thinking I'm the one using the Presidential Suite.

Astrid moves silently beside me as we exit the kitchen, cross the living area, and enter the hallway where she stood, getting to know more about me than she wanted to. I want to pressure her to answer me, but I keep quiet and convince myself that I'm content with just escorting her past the family photos of Natalia, Luke, and Luke Jr. that are mounted on sage green walls.

My familiarity with the house and Astrid's perfect recall takes us in the direction of the nursery and master bedroom, where her clothes are folded neatly on the bed. I should be going in the opposite way toward the guest bedrooms that haven't been transformed into children's rooms yet.

At the opened mahogany door is an unobstructed view of the sun-filled bedroom with a massive bed, it's floral bedspread, a mountain range's worth of pillows, and a lumpy, square patch of white that is Astrid's dress. She stops in the doorway, drops her hand from my arm, and turns to me. The absence of her touch leaves me wanting it back desperately, but encroaching on her personal bubble seems like a bad idea at the moment.

"Blake, I just need a little time to get used to... everything. We've never lived together, dated, or hell, talked as much as we have in the last few hours about anything."

God, if she's backing out on giving me the next month to prove myself, I swear I'll scream like a girl, or drop down to my knees and beg her to stay.

Things will get highly awkward after I finish doing either one and possibly make her feel even more uptight around me. My mind scrambles to come up with another method that gives her the space, which she obviously needs, to come to terms with our new but wobbly relationship. I just need to keep her in my territory. It doesn't take long for an idea to form.

"You don't have to move in with me, Astrid. You can get your old apartment back in town, or a new one. The old one is still empty though, since old man Sampson is doing some remodeling to it, but I can use my influence to get you in the new high rise condominiums a few miles away, tonight. They come fully furnished."

90

This will be the first thing that my parents own that might actually benefit me, and I can't be happier that they're branching out into real estate in their golden years. Not glad about having to ask them for a favor. For Astrid, I'll confront an approaching a snake about to strike. The Powers are in the same category.

Getting them to lease me an apartment in Powers' Court won't be difficult at all since they want something from me, and it's only a few miles away from my much less expensive residence.

She raises an eyebrow. "I don't think I can afford a new high rise condominium. My savings will probably run out after I give a deposit and the first month's rent."

"Astrid, when I said I'd support you, I meant I'd support you in every way. Since I asked you to stay, I should pay for it."

Her mouth opens, probably to refuse me, her independent streak a mile wide just like Malisa's used to be. I set my mouth lightly down on hers, not giving her the chance to speak. When her lips pucker beneath mine, clearly participating in the kiss, I hope I've found a technique to get my way with her too; my touch. I'll never make her regret it, or take it for granted again. But just in case I haven't located her soft spot yet, I tilt my head, resting my forehead on hers. I'm not above using skin contact to remind her of what we used to have. My family's future together under one roof hangs on it.

"Let me do this for you, sweetheart, at least for my son. If we don't work out, and I wouldn't bank on that if I was you, you'll still have your savings to get a place whenever you decide to move out from your parents.' I don't think you'll want to stay with them and raise our child. You've always struck me as a woman who enjoys her space." Or she'd have asked me to commit to her long before now.

Hell, she still hasn't asked. I'm asking her.

The corners of her mouth curve upward in my downward view. "I don't need that much space, Blake," she says huskily.

I don't have to be a rocket scientist or be looking in her face to know what she means; she's about to take what she wants from me. The only problem is, where will I let her remove it from me at?

"Astrid, as much as I love making love with you, and *need* to do it right now, I don't think we should piss off Uncle Luke by sleeping in his bed. *Any* of them. He's an ex-boxer who breaks big ass horses so little children can ride them, and I don't have my gun."

Quiet hilarity climbs out of her throat. "Blake, obviously, you've never used a bathroom for more than its original purpose."

The stiffness in my pants presses at the seam again. Adrenaline roils through me like a swarm of bees that have been disturbed, and they're angry. The risks from disrespecting Uncle Luke's home slides to the deepest, darkest crevices of my mind and quickly forgotten about. My cock is straight pussy-whipped.

Just your cock, huh?

I grab Astrid's hand and lead the way past the bed, where I snatch up her dress, before continuing to the ensuite bathroom several feet away. I can't get there fast enough. She's right on my heels.

"I'm starting to think you like seducing me in places you shouldn't, Astrid."

"What? You don't like doing risky things with me anymore?" she taunts.

"This isn't risky, baby. This is suicidal, and Uncle Luke will be glad to kill me for it, and you're an adrenaline junkie."

"I don't have to worry about him killing me too though, right?"

"Nope, but I'll probably die twice at his hands for your part in this, so I better not mention that this is *your* idea." Dying one time is one too damn many already.

"As long as baby Blake and I are good then I promise to miss you when you're gone."

I step onto white, marble squares with tan grout, then swing around in front of his and her sinks encased in teakwood, to face Astrid. I lay her dress down on the surface between the porcelain basins and tug on the bowtie, unravelling the ends of it. "You know that is the second time you were willing to sacrifice me to my family. I'm starting to worry."

She releases my hand, backs up, and reaches for the door blindly. While pushing it closed with her fingertips, she slides a braided strap off her shoulder. "I promise to make it worth your while, while you're living."

"You always damn do, and that's why I'm your sucker."

"But you're a gorgeous sucker that I can't resist, that's for sure."

"Oh, is that right?"

She nods.

"Well that makes dying worth it then." I shrug out of my coat, so the floor can have its turn at wearing it, while watching her slip the other strap off her shoulder. They start to slide down her arms out of sync, releasing her breasts one plump mound at a time. Much bigger than a handful now, her nipples darker and engorged like overripe plums. I wonder if they still taste sweet. My mouth waters, while my eyes drift down her body, taking in every inch of uncovered skin left vulnerable by her top falling away.

It gathers beneath her stomach. I stop tracking her flesh to gawk at her naked, stretched abdomen. I've never seen a more beautiful sight than my child rounding out her body, and it chokes me up, again.

Now, where the hell is my best man? That's right, you don't have one yet, so you'll have to check your own damn emotions, Blake.

"Blake," Astrid calls softly, "you're thinking too much."

I clear my throat loudly and focus on her hands nudging her clothing downward. The outfit drops to the floor, becoming a puddle at her feet. She steps out of it unhurriedly. My mind is equally slow to register that I still have too many damn clothes on, and I'm far behind Astrid, who's walking toward me in just her birthday suit. Where in the hell is her underwear? The answer becomes a nonfactor when urgency to be just as bare ass as she is slams into my gut.

Her gaze is hotter than a five-alarm blaze on my face, and I need the frigid air pumping from the vents overhead to hit directly on every inch of me. I yank the lilac bowtie loose. She reaches me, both hands angle my neck downward, so she can sip from my lips, but battling, not dancing, is

Astrid's favorite way to kiss. She quickly takes it there, the slow winding of our mouths lasting only seconds. My hand stretches out to drop the piece of formal scrap of cotton from my neck on top of her dress laying on the countertop.

I unhook the cummerbund dyed to match the bowtie perfectly and toss it to the floor. Her fingers skim down to my neck, where she starts on my shirt buttons. I jerk on the one for my pants. It bounces across the floor. I'll have to reimburse Malisa for the repair, since the tux is a rental. It'll be the best money I ever spent.

Warm puffs of Astrid's breath fan against the naked skin on my chest peeking out from the opened ends of my shirt, raising my body temperature a little higher. At this rate, I'll need an ice bath to cool down. She drags a blunt nail down my pectoral. It swerves around my nipple and abs onto the happy trail of fine hair that doesn't end at my brief's waistband. Neither does her fingertip.

Inside my pants, she fists my length. I buck forward in her hand, and begin to go quietly loco. Ravenous hunger to caress her everywhere takes up residence where my appetite for food should be. Six months of not making love with her is turning me into a beast, but there's no way in hell I'll spread Astrid on the cold floor just to feast on her body. I'm going to have to go hungry a little longer, until I can get her to a bedroom.

"Jesus, Astrid, when will we ever make it to a bed like a regular couple?" I ask gruffly.

She tucks her tongue between her teeth. Her fingers spread flat across the space between my stomach and my hips, then skates upwards, scrubbing the tails of my shirt out of my pants. Her head lifts, eyes boring into mine. "If I promise we'll find a bed really, really soon, will you stop snipping at me because I need you when I need you? I've gone a long time without you."

The unmistakable desire in her tone ratchets up my optimism for having a life with Astrid, where choosing fast and wild sex over slow and meaningful making love will be in a long line of the sacrifices that I'll happily make. I'll give anything to wake up next to this woman every morning, and have already slaked my lust for her the night before so I'm not inviting certain death at the hands of my uncle. Rushing through sex with her in inappropriate places before we get caught used to be the highlight of my days, and nothing will get more unfitting than a room belonging to Uncle Luke, who could knock down the door to this one at any time.

Astrid is all I need to get my blood pumping, and sometimes, a man likes to take his time with his woman. She has new dimensions to her body that I want to explore. Undoubtedly, she has new sensitive zones originating from her pregnancy than just the ones behind her ears, neck, and between her breasts. Just breathing on them seems to turn her inside out and make her cry out.

Yeah, I should definitely stay away from those spots right now.

"Fine," I say grumpily and back away, while pushing my slacks and underwear down, "but you're riding me while I sit on the toilet." Every step I take back, she takes forward, with a cute and smug smirk on her mouth, a gleam in her eyes. I'd think she's a predator, if she wasn't smiling.

"Deal, cowboy," she agrees readily, because she'll take the lead in all our lovemaking sessions if I let her, and I often do, getting the chance to watch her get lost in the enjoyment she finds in my body. I haven't gotten enough of that yet, probably won't.

When my calves finally collide with the side of the commode, I reach back and close the lid, then take a sit down on it, wanting more than my next breath to browse her curves, arches, nooks, and crannies just to relearn them. Instead, my hands cheerfully pitch upwards for her waist. Bracing her weight while she swings her legs on each side of mine makes the apex of her thighs a target for the heat-seeking missile standing erect between mine. All my body parts seem to be reacting to her as if her body is a magnet, and they're powerfully attracted, which hasn't changed in the time she's been gone.

She squats over my lap, and eases down until the tip of my penis is touching her distended clitoris. She jerks upwards, as if the skin to skin contact between us burns her. Then she comes back for more, which is brutal on my senses. I shut my eyes, and pray for strength to not cum quick like an overeager teenager before I'm in her. When she swivels her hips, my shaft invades her wet folds, positioning perfectly at her soaking wet entrance. The base of my spine tingles and my toes curl in my shoes.

It looks like I should be worrying more about lasting long enough to get her off than caught. She moans above me and dips down, taking half of me inside. It no longer matters that we're reconnecting in a bathroom anymore. All I know is that I have the staggering feeling of coming home finally. Now how in the hell do I make her feel this way too, without coercing her, before my time is up at the end of the month?

Unaware of my inner skirmishes, Astrid throws her head back on her shoulders, sinks her nails into mine, and drops down until she's fully seated in my lap. Fire licks through my middle and takes my breath away. Baby Blake's shelter is also pressing into my middle unforgivingly, which has to be uncomfortable for everyone. Before I can express my concern about that, Astrid glides backwards along my thighs, lessening my penetration in her body. That damn sure isn't going to work. I need her to be completely impaled by me. With my hands still gripping her waist, I scoot forward without warning.

The sudden movement makes Astrid squeal and lace her fingers behind my neck tightly, with her tiptoes scrubbing the floor. "What are you doing?"

"Just hold on. I got you, love."

I adjust my body on the seat some more. She snorts, highly amused. Finally, I find a much more comfortable spot for us all, with my spine laying along the cold porcelain lid with my ass hanging off the edge, so she's leaning over me while balancing on my legs. Her hands slip from around my neck, to plant palms down in my chest. She raises up so she's straddling me, puts her feet firmly down on the floor, and smirks at me.

"Maybe this isn't such a good idea, Blake."

I can understand why she may be changing her mind; eight months ago, she and I were a perfect fit while sitting up. "I have no problems with making room for my son. Trying new positions keeps the fire from dying in a relationship… or so I've heard. And these thighs can take any motion you feel like doing."

She cackles loudly above me. "Oh, I have no doubts about your thighs. They're muscular enough to choke a tree, and this is definitely a new position for us, especially in a bathroom… but I like it. Weirdly, it seems more intimate than anything we've ever done." It is for me, too.

I've never taken her body with the intention of gaining her heart before, or tried to find where I fit in her world on her terms, which hopefully meshes with mine soon. The urgent need to thrust up and reclaim some of the ground that I lost in her takes over me. I go with it. Her hips rock forward, meeting me halfway, and then rotate in a circle. A groan erupts from deep in her throat, a hushed 'yes.' With her sweet spot successfully found, I feel the compulsion to gently persuade her to my side of the current situation that's standing between us like a massive wall. Only she can knock it down.

"Imagine what else I can make work for us three, Astrid."

Her eyes soften. "I am, Blake. God knows I am."

"Exactly what I wanted to hear. That's enough pressuring you for now. Let's see if you can still ride me like you used to." Challenge issued, I watch her shut her eyes then push off with her hands, to grind on the tip of my shaft imbedded in her soft tissue, which is radiating warmth like she carries an inferno around within her.

Friction from her body milking my base begins to scramble my dedication to make this moment long enough to be a beloved memory of hers. Her snug tunnel tests my strength to resist finishing before she does. She's like my own personal hell.

I can't believe I was stupid enough to let it get away.

"You need to hurry, Blake," she pants, while working her body in slow, erotic moves meant to make a man cum.

"Actually, I should probably just lay here, baby." I have to force the words through gritted teeth.

"Blake, I'll cum without you, I swear," she moans, as if she's in pain.

"That's the plan, darling. Now cum for me."

My hands drive her down, making her take most of me. Her body clamps around mine. Pressure mounts in my testicles. The need to explode increases by a hundred notches. My hips lunge upwards without my consent this time, submerging my shaft deeper inside her body. It's exactly where every part of me wants to be. Then she hisses. I freeze in place.

"Too deep, baby?"

Her forehead wrinkles up. "Yes... no. Shit, I don't know." Good. If she's overwhelmed, she can't think about anything to do with leaving me.

"Then I'll stay right where I am." I'm positive that's one of my better ideas. Besides, if I move again, this quickie will be over.

"Fine by me, babe." She continues to coil her body, moan softly, and squeeze her inner muscles together until I can't think of anything but detonating inside her.

"Fuck, Astrid," I grunt and shove further up into her, to escape the oven-like temperature in her body that is cooking my willpower. Completely groggy-minded, pulling out of her never even occurs to me. I wouldn't have anyway.

"You *are* fucking me, baby, and it's been too damn long," she wails on a downshift.

"That's for damn sure, but you're fucking *me* senseless. Hurry up and cum before I have to write you an IOU."

Her fingers tunnel into my chest until her nails are scraping the flesh. Thank God she doesn't have claws, or she'd be ripping me apart right now, a sure sign that she's getting closer to her release. The minute pain mixed with extreme pleasure is enough to make me go mad and keep me somewhat rational at the same time.

Her head lulls between her shoulder blades, as her pace picks up. Her thighs slap against mine. Juices run down the back of my penis. A mantra of soundless curse words break from her lips. Her losing control is the only thing that keeps me from falling over the edge. It's too damn fascinating to not look at her while she loses herself with me inside her, or what's left of my right mind would have faded away long before now.

"Blake," she whispers, my signal to fuck her back, topping from the bottom.

Before she finishes saying my name, my hips are already swinging up. Astrid's knees rise, drawing together to rest on my sides. Gripping the globes of her ass, I boost her up. Two short pumps send us both freefalling. My fingers cramp around her flesh, naturally seeking an anchor to the earth while my senses rocket to the four corners of the room. I have to force myself to let her waist go, before every muscle in my body clenches up under the pressure of my climax that's rocking me from the inside out.

"Oh fuck!" She balls up on herself.

I pick one hand up off the floor to cover her mouth, while my body releases every ounce of my seed into her.

"Astrid! Blake!" Uncle Luke yells back. "Is everything okay?"

Well, shit!

Chapter Seven

Blake

Astrid's head snaps upright, eyes jerking downward to me. She's horrified, but her body ripples around mine, still orgasming while I need to think quick on my feet… uh, back. My first impulse is to stomp my foot on the floor.

"It's okay, baby! It's just a spider!" I say loudly.

Now, I must keep up the pretense of rats *and* spiders being in places that they're not. Natalia uses a homemade organic insect and rodent repellent around the house, which is also edible and safe for Luke Jr. I even use it at the station.

Astrid giggles behind my hand. Her eyes get watery.

"Blake," Uncle Luke's tone is extremely sarcastic, "you'll have to come up with a better lie than that, and there better not be any of your babies on my floor, tub, sink, toilet. God forbid my towels or I swear—"

"We're still changing, Uncle Luke," I interrupt, before he can get completely worked up, feeling like a child again. I was always getting into trouble for something I usually dragged Malisa into, until I wised up at the ripe old age of ten. "I probably carried the spider in from outside on my clothes."

"If anything, you're the spider that convinced Astrid to be your waterspout. Use the towels under the sink to clean up with. Not those hanging for decoration on the bar in front of the toilet or behind it. Put yours straight in the washing machine. If Natalia tells me that—"

"It's all good, Uncle Luke. We don't need towels. I swear," I lie. "We'll be out in a minute."

I reach over with my free hand and flush the toilet. "All gone, Astrid. You can step out of the tub now."

She pushes my hand down her chin. "Thank you, Blake," she says weakly, as if she's really at the back of the bathroom, recoiling in the whirlpool and terrified.

Then, a riot of chuckles quietly discharge from her. She replaces my fingers over her lips and laughs so hard behind them, silently. Her chest is heaving. Baby Blake is probably getting seasick. I want this to be a memory that she wouldn't forget, but *neither* of us is ever going to.

"One minute, Blake," Uncle Luke warns. "I'll be back. The reception starts as soon as they finish setting up the food, and you two better be there. Malisa will make us wait for you if you aren't, and I'm starving." Right. Bear, no porridge.

"Okay, Astrid has to use the bathroom first. She didn't get a chance when we got here." When did I sink to bargaining for time to hide my bad judgment calls from my uncle?

A long time ago, Blake, and you haven't made that many right ones before today. At least, I'm making love to Astrid inside a real relationship, so I'm doing better, dammit!

I set Astrid on her feet quickly, and whisper, "We have to move, love. He means it."

I reach for the closest cabinet door beneath the sinks and pluck two hand towels with shredded ends from the top of a neatly folded stack with various sizes.

Astrid takes them from my hand, points at my lap, indicating I should keep my seat. She wets the towels before soaping them up with a rose-scented soap that Natalia always smells like, rinses them, and tosses one to me. "You only have time to wipe up. I owe you a bath when we get back to your place."

Nerves, which I didn't know were shaken, settle inside me when she names the next pit stop in our world. "Thank you, Astrid," I say, then proceed to clean her essence off my lap and enormously contented man parts.

She may never know what I'm truly thanking her for. I don't part with the knowledge because I truly want it to be her decision to stay with me. Sentimental words tend to make a woman stick around for sentimental reasons, which only last for so long before she realizes her mistake. I want her to stay because it's what she undoubtedly wants.

We make our wash-ups quick. Astrid shimmers into her underwear and shoves her dress over her head. Lucky her; I forgot to bring my change of clothes with me, and need to move now. I put back on my suit, scoop up her wet towel along with mine, and hurry toward the closed closet door right behind the bathroom's. Inside are more towels sitting on shelves, but I only need two that's identical to the ones we used.

"You are devious as hell, Blake," Astrid cracks, with a small smile in her voice from behind me while I squat down in front of the cabinet.

"You're talking to the kid that got away with more shit than he got punished for," I say as I replace the towels then smooth out the folds. "This is how I got away with it. Leave as little evidence behind as possible. Suspicions amount to about the same thing with family and a court of law; don't mean shit unless you got absolute proof. Well, that's how it's supposed to go in a court of law anyway. As long as I excluded Malisa from my misbehaving, I came out smelling like... damn... roses."

Astrid howls with laughter, catching onto the irony right away. "We're both smelling like roses right now."

"Exactly." If Uncle Luke doesn't demand to smell my crotch, I should get away scot free with taking advantage of privacy with Astrid in his home and the whopper I gave him about not needing to clean up. And, so help me God, I will learn to resist Astrid until I can get her home.

I don't think Astrid will tell anyone about this time though. She'll be snitching on herself, as well.

After I'm sure the towels look the very same way as I found the others, I stand up to open the bathroom door and surveil the bedroom, half expecting Uncle Luke to still be standing guard in it. He isn't. I turn back to Astrid to peck her on the forehead.

"Go to the kitchen. On the other side of the table is a pantry door in the corner of the room. Natalia has empty shopping bags on the middle shelf. Grab one for the wet towels and bring it to me in the bedroom at the end of the hall. See you in a minute, lady."

Then I damn near run to the guest bedroom that has my extra set of clothes and Uncle Tommy's only a few yards away. It feels like a mile. This wouldn't be necessary if Malisa had trusted the men to remember to bring their formalwear from home. Instead, she held the tuxedos hostage at Uncle Luke's ranch, and we all had to change here. Having luck that sucks is the reason why Uncle Tommy and I got the changing area farthest away from the master's bathroom.

Leaving the door open to make it easy for Astrid to find me, I toss the towels on the gray carpet beside the bed and begin to strip as if my life depends on it. It probably does if I don't get to the reception in time. Layers of my suit land all over the place as I rush to undress. Toeing my shoes off, a cool draft on my back precedes Astrid entering the room. A soft click resonates when she closes the door. In my side vision, pieces of my suit start to fly through the air once again, becoming a pile beside two garment bags laying on the striped gray and black quilt.

I spin around in my briefs and socks. "Sweetheart, I got that. Take a seat and enjoy. This is the only striptease you're going to get from me."

She shakes her head, and snickers quietly before picking up a black oxford loafer with a monk-strap. "I'm not helpless, Blake, and I got us in this shit so I'm helping you out of it. It's fine for me to bend over, I just can't stretch too far up… but don't make this picking up after you a habit, grown man. Anything that lands on the ceiling fan is on you, grown man or not," she jests, as I snatch my white tee from the bed over my head.

I hop into the loose fit jeans next. "Got it." And whatever the hell else she needs, even if I have to break a law to get it. "Trust me, I am not making any of this a habit. We make a deal right now to wait until we're in our own home to make love."

The plastic bag in her hand crinkles as she shoves the wet towels into them. I don't even bother to tie up my khaki boots, after thrusting my feet into them. No time. Pulling the strings tight, stuffing them in my shoes, and covering up the rush job with my jeans is going to have to do. When done, I stand up, with no amen from Astrid about practicing self-preservation around Uncle Luke's home or anyone else's establishment, especially when the owner is as heavily-muscled as I am and he has a history of knocking unarmed people the hell out in boxing rings for fun. I highly doubt if that's why she's hesitating to seal the bargain though—I fucked up big time when I let 'our own home' dribble out of my mouth.

"Astrid, sweetheart, I know you love my body and all, but it may get us killed if we're caught even one time making up for lost time," I joke, somewhat, to take her mind off my screw up of giving her glimpse into what I want our lives could be.

She doesn't even look back. Unease slithers through me when I can't find the right words to tease her out of her mood. I always could before, but this isn't 'before,' and I can't help but to think that I'm really running out of time. Well, I am, but soothing Astrid means much more than hearing the groom wish himself a lifelong marriage, no matter how bad Uncle Luke wants to eat.

"Astrid, I didn't mean we had to have our own home right now… if ever," I add for her benediction, but I'm fucking petrified that it might just go down that way.

I get no response. Mentally, I'm treading on a thin ledge with a steep drop off, and I can't see the bottom. Her chin plummets into her chest, whenever she wants to avoid something. That's not often, so I always take notice.

She finally sits down on the farthest corner of the bed. A canyon opens up between us. The light atmosphere turns dark and heavy. She inhales deeply, as if she's trying to get a control of her emotions. I guess we're both freaking out right now.

"Are you done dressing yet?" she asks hoarsely, then reaches back for the heap of clothes.

She scoots them closer. I wait for her to acknowledge me with her eyes. Instead, she concentrates on filling the closest garment bag sprawled out behind her, making sure nothing gets snagged on the zipper, tucking the missing pants button and silk pocket square in the breast pocket. Handling dirty laundry doesn't take that much effort. She's been hesitating to bind herself to anything with me on the other end of it since she got here.

There isn't a thing I can do about it or the giant leaps we're taking backwards after making baby steps forward together.

What if she never wants a 'together?'

It takes all the strength I have to not go to her. Touching her is like breathing, ingrained.

I stroke my jaw to give my hands something to do.

"Astrid, I'm not trying to talk you into something that you don't want. If you don't want to move in with me right now, just say so, so I can get you in your own apartment right away. It won't change how I feel about you, you know?"

Finally, she glances back. "You sure?"

Bingo.

I'm not sure exactly what part of my statement her question is pertaining to, but she's talking again and looking at me. I'll take that over her moodiness any day. I can't stop a deep-seated surge that's driving me near her, to protect her and create a stress-free bubble while feeling our way towards reconciling. I kneel before her, clutching my thighs to keep from putting my hands on hers.

"I'm sure. I've waited twenty-six years for you. I think I can wait until you're sure about me too… however long it takes. Did you bring any luggage with you?"

She nods her head. "I didn't know if I'd track you down right away, but I planned for a week's stay if I needed to be here that long." A trace of leeriness swims in her eyes.

Damn.

When she's not craving my body, my closeness is a real issue for her. I vow to make it bearable until she craves that, too, which means not sticking closely until she wants me to. I take the sack with the towels balled in her lap from her. Knotting it up, I rise to my feet, and hurl it toward the top of the tall boy chest of drawers set against the right-side wall. The majestic crown molding on top almost scrapes the ceiling, and it's a childhood hiding place for things I don't want anyone to find. Haven't used it in years.

Astrid's head shadows the arc of the bag until it's out of sight, then her gaze swivels back to me. "What are you doing with those towels?"

"Putting them out of sight until I leave tonight, then taking them home and washing them. Washing them here will be all Uncle Luke needs to be right about what we were doing in his bathroom. We don't want him to be right. I'll bring them back tomorrow." I stretch my fingers to hers, to help her up. "Okay. I'll take you back to the reception, then make calls about getting you a place after Apollo gives his best man speech."

She smiles and lets my hand gulp hers. "That toast is going to be entertaining."

"Damn near everything that goes on with the family is."

When she's on her feet, I back up and let her go, hardest thing I ever had to do. I don't want her to know that though, so I return her grin with something splitting apart in my chest. Realization, that I could really lose Astrid before I can rightfully call her mine, leaks out of the hole and pools in the pit of my midsection like dead weight.

Since she's still skittish as hell around me, I'll just have to hold onto the belief that we'll survive this together for the both...make that *three* of us. It's going to be hell sleeping in my bed alone, knowing she's so close but couldn't be farther away. I'll do it for her though.

****

Astrid

Walking in front of Blake, I feel like I'm on a goddamn yo-yo that's constantly being launched outward. Scared. Holding on tight to what is tangible, which is the string I'm pirouetting on. My inability to let go of it and leap into a new way of being with Blake has him spinning with me, back and forth, out of control. It's plain as day that he's trying to find the middle ground between offering me a way off the tumultuous ride and being considerate of my feelings while I gain confidence in him and poise in myself again.

In the meantime, I'm confusing him. Hell, I'm confused, and it's inducing misery for the both of us. His is given away by the draining of happiness from his eyes and the slump of his shoulders every time I accept his affections then draw back from him. I can't help it. There's an ache deep inside forged from the time we spent apart that he made no moves to correct until after I'd come to him. It's preventing me from surrendering to him fully again, a mistake I made the first time when he wouldn't let me in.

Now, he's doing everything in his power to be the man I want, making me feel cherished. He did that before, when I knew better than to read anything more into it. The pretty words out of his mouth are nice this go around, but I'm petrified that he'll take back anything he's said to me today. I don't know this Blake. God knows I want to, even while catapulting through midair. Body constantly fighting me to snatch moments of intimacy with him. He's as addicting as heroin. Withdrawal is horrendous. Keeps me awake most nights in Harrison until I fall asleep, exhausted and all cried out from missing his body next to mine. Whenever he's near me, the pleasure center in my brain demands I find a way in his arms and get a hit of his body.

Why couldn't it be just me who'll be deceived by Blake's promises of love if they prove to be false? A second chance to be with him would already be in the works, parents called and told to ship my possessions back here. Baby Blake must be my first priority now, and I'll be damned if he gets hurt because I'm an addict and his father is my choice of drug. Blake and I are just going to hold on a little bit longer during the yo-yoing until I can find my way back to the woman I used to be with him.

I don't reach back for his hand though I want to. His touch blinds me to his faults. He doesn't offer his touch, staying a step behind, eyes tunneling into the space within my shoulder blades and creating a continuous tingle there. The remoteness between us is good for my mind that's comfortable with it after all the time we've spent apart, while the core of me screams for the man that's turned my body against me. Our excursion across the property to the tract for the after-wedding festivities is filled with screeching silence. Baby Blake presses on my spine as if he's trying to get to his father, even if I'm not.

He's been shifting to whatever side Blake is on since his father stroked my stomach. Already a daddy's boy. What if I'm depriving my child of someone he seems to require in his life before he's even born? I have no way of knowing, no guarantees to put the blame on if nothing pans out in Arrow. My broken heart is one thing, my child's another. Self-preservation says to just give it time… this time.

Blake and mini-him deserve it and are worth it.

In the distance, a miniature open-ended maze of compact lush leaves vastly outnumbering their lilac blooms begins to block out the cloudless sky. In its absence, the sun lends its radiance to the surroundings. The scenic view of mountains peek over the border of hedgerows doubling as the horizon.

Malisa couldn't have picked a more spectacular place to tie her life to someone she loves in front of those she loved first. The beauty of the landscape and this momentous day wars with my blues.

You will not fucking cry right now, Astrid. Your wedding day will come… someday. Yeah, that makes me feel better.

A soft breeze steals every other word out of energetic chatter, music lyrics, and animated resonance from children's play, transporting them to us. Everyone's elation is almost palpable.

As we get closer to it, tinkling sounds of dishes rise in volume. I pursue the noise until crystal bowls with floating petals and unlit tealights dotting the middle of rectangular lavender tablecloths come into view. Most of the ladder back chairs are empty. The people assigned to them are in line at the buffet, conversing and waiting to be served, or at the bar on the other side.

Malisa waves us over to a table running parallel with the backside of the enclosure. A cardboard assembly of realistic silver thrones envelop her and Apollo's seats. Behind them, Maria is losing the fight with a net full of balloons trying to soar away before it is time. Above her, a soft breeze is aggravating the sheer, white panel scarf with drooping cascades segregated by silver medallions. They're miraculously rigged to the highest point of the foliage, adding style and grace to the setting. I can't be accused of having either now, and need a minute to pull myself together.

"Blake, go see what she wants. I'll find a seat that isn't taken and wait for you to come find me after the last toast... or during the dance. Whatever comes first."

He shakes his head. "Keep moving, Astrid. I doubt if Malisa wants me seated at the bride and groom's table. If she does and you're not welcome, which I highly doubt, I'm still not sitting up there without you."

"It's fine if she does." I'm barely a guest, but he's family. "I can sit with the guests. Everything should be the way she wants it on her day." I'm not about to spawn discord in his family relations over the seating arrangement.

Phantom fingertips bump against the base of my backbone, and linger. Blake's intense presence converges with mine from behind.

"Move, Astrid," he commands right against my ear.

I shiver. For a moment, my woes roll away. This man's touch and nearness is everything.

Of course, it is, that's why you don't want it on you until you know for sure if he'll still want you tomorrow... and the day after that... and the day... I get it. Damn! Lay off, conscious.

115

Finally, we're standing before Malisa's and Apollo's joyful faces. She's more than gorgeous in her diamond-studded wedding dress, thick, jet-black ringlets spread-out on her shoulders. Her makeup consists of mascara and gloss, just the right amount I'd select for myself. Mixing with her is hard when she's so happy, and I'm tainted with misgivings and fears... oh, and envy.

This could be my day if Blake and I had done things right from the very beginning. Working at another department, unbothered about who'll discover the true nature of our association, wouldn't have been a tribulation, as long as I was coming home to him every night.

You came home to him almost every morning, and things still fell apart.

A repeat of that would break me.

Which is why you're running scared, even while standing still.

As if it isn't bad enough that I know my shortcomings, I'm chunking them at myself internally too, and hitting all the weakest spots. What I wouldn't do for blissful ignorance again.

"About time you two made it," Malisa chirps then sips from a flute of water, her eyes flit over the rim to the far end of the bride's section. "Sit on my side of the table, and you'll have some privacy to talk while everyone eats before they converge on the newest members of the family."

Damn, I'm not even with Blake and she's already calling me family. The back of my eyes burn. *You. Will. Not. Cry, Astrid, dammit! Now say thank you, because you're not fit to meet anyone right now.*

"Thank you, Malisa," I manage throatily.

"Anytime, sister." She winks and replaces her goblet on the table.

I feel a tug in my chest and must inhale around the nub suddenly in my throat just to breathe. Apollo leans over to kiss the top of her head. Blake's fingers prod me to sidestep. I revolve toward the bride's corner, to circle the table, stopping behind two empty chairs with preset place settings of pyramid-shaped napkins, prefilled wine and water glasses, and utensils. There aren't any on the groom's side however.

"Smells like a setup, doesn't it?" Blake mumbles, drawing a harrumph out of me.

"Yep."

But it's just family looking out for family. It'll be easy to grow attached to Malisa. With her forethought, she's making her home a home away from home for me, and I am grateful.

He pulls the inner chair out for me. "Sit, and I'll get you something to eat. Preferential treatment will get me ahead of the line."

"Or you'll start whining that you are white and adopted?"

He shrugs arrogantly. "That, or I'll remind everyone that I have a starving, pregnant lady to take care of."

Mounting giggles make me toss my head back to release them. "No shame, Blake."

"Nope. Be right back."

I spy on his departure openly, couldn't have looked away if I wanted to. His gait is long. Back straight. Head held high. Inner strength evident in the way he conveys himself.

Lord, that man has swag.

Out of all the girls in the world, why did he choose me? There's no wonder why my body keeps choosing him back. He's the full package, handsome, hardworking, and more than capable in the bedroom, but with imperfections that may become deal breakers. I won't know if they are until I know everything there is to know about him.

And that's your problem. You don't know enough yet.

That's the kink in my chain. While I'm working it out, I'm holding back, jerking us around, and hurting us even when I know what I want. Blake, always him, even if he has a million obstacles around him. I just need to know what course to plot. Is that too much to ask?

True to his word, he acquires two overloaded platters and makes his way back to me in no time. I hide a grin. No matter where we're at, he takes care of my creature comforts first. He halts before me, setting down the plates loaded down with baked fish, seafood, barbequed ribs, and steamed vegetables.

"We're sharing," he mentions before taking the seat beside me.

"I would hope so. This is too much even for someone who's eating for two."

"For four." He pats his stomach then scoots closer to me, always a big eater.

Our own little bubble starts to grow around us, permeated with exclusiveness from everyone else.

Intimacy.

I inhale it, summoning recollections of taking breaks together at work that left the world behind, or we shut it out completely when he visited me at my home on my days off.

Fuck!

Blake is adept at creating this environment, and it tramples the guards around my heart no matter what I resurrect them out of, or when.

I clear my throat and try to disengage from him by eyeing the food and sucking up less of the sensuality impregnating the invisible closed-off section.

"This is more like for six, Blake."

"Leftovers, Astrid," he says patronizingly with a crooked grin. "Ever heard of them?"

"Yes, but I have a feeling there aren't going to be any."

He filches a rib and takes a big bite. "Probably not. Eat up. Mama O puts her foot in everything she cooks, and we have a growing boy who will love her for it."

"And he's sitting between us right now, mashing my left lung," I complain. The baby squirms against my rib cage, which will be sore tomorrow if he does that enough times.

Blake cocks an eyebrow, pride flickering in his bright blues. "So he knows his daddy's voice already, huh?" Arrogant as hell, but I've given him something to be pleased about again. That's a plus after being a killjoy repeatedly.

I smirk and spoon baked salmon and asparagus into my mouth. "I'm surprised you didn't deny he's yours." I don't know the dynamics of

Blake's bond with his blood family, but working in Arrow takes me into homes of people that live for gossip. The Powers are millionaires that don't have one-black girl or mixed heritage member in their lineage, and don't want any. The circuit court's Judge Adrian is sleeping with his secretary, allegedly. The list goes on and on.

"Astrid, you're not scheming and manipulative like that."

"How do you know?"

Blake's jaw fills out as his tongue scrapes the inside of it. "Because I know you, woman."

"So, why did you think you couldn't confide in me about your issues?"

Heaviness pushes into bubble. Blake turns to me, while chewing slowly.

"I didn't want you to face what everyone would think if I told you that you and Malisa could pass for sisters. She's a big part of my life, and certain people with sensitive information can connect the dots about my feelings for her at one point and you. I don't know who all has that information, but Malisa once said I'm destined to end up in my own handcuffs, and I will if someone approaches you with some bullshit about your resemblance."

Connect the dots, huh?

My eyes fall to the table, appetite waning. I lay my spoon beside the plate, slowly. "So do you still have a thing for your sister? Even remotely?"

His answer could qualify as a deal breaker and more heartache rolled into one, but I want to know the basic details anyway.

Chapter Eight

Blake

"*Had* a thing, as a teenager," I respond quickly, while looking directly in her eyes, giving her access to my soul. Should've done it long ago. "For about a week. Never acted on it. Don't think I missed out on anything, but I'm not blind to her inner beauty, what makes her a good woman, and her faults. She has plenty of them, but she's the type of woman I knew I wanted in my life even as a boy, so I used her as a mirror to hold other women up to when I started dating. Hadn't met one that measured up before *you*. I just didn't expect to find a woman that not only carries herself like Malisa and works as damn hard as she does, but looks so damn much like her too, which doesn't matter as long as there's a good heart beneath the looks. Speaking of hearts, you almost gave mine an attack when I first saw you. There was never a moment I confused you with her. Your differences from her fucked with my mind and body big time. I knew you were going to be a distraction the moment I saw you, and I was right. The council wouldn't send you back to Harrison and I got stuck with falling in love with you."

She snorts and picks her spoon back up, and begins to shake her head. "I never knew that."

I take a deep breath, glad to see that I only killed her ability to eat temporarily. "It never dawned on me that I'd create a whole other set of problems with you by keeping my own counsel either. Yes, I should've told you everything at the beginning of our relationship, how much I wanted to protect you... from *everything*. I fell in love with you almost fucking immediately. All I had to do was look at you to know where I was headed, head over damn heels. Obviously, my hindsight is much better than my vision. I didn't keep quiet about us just because of Malisa and my parents though. I didn't want to hurt your career either. It means so much to you, so it means that much to me, too. Now, why did you just up and leave me? I haven't gotten a good day's sleep since, even after I drove to your parents to make sure you were okay and safe."

Her mouth falls open.

I can't help wallowing in the shock waves running rampant in her face, and proving her wrong about something; she was never just a convenient fuck for me. "Yes, Astrid. I knew where were you, but I'm not a stalker. Well, not much of one anyway. I only drove to Harrison a few times in the first week you left... like every day, and parked down the street in a rental car. Didn't feel like even a tenth of a man until I saw you sitting on the screen porch with your mother sipping coffee in the cold mornings. Then I stopped myself from going to Harrison. It was either that or beg you to come back home. I still had crap hanging like an executioner's sword over my head, so I let you be until I could break out from under it all."

123

A heavy exhalation leaves her. Her neck starts to work overtime, as if she's having to consume her emotions. "You were coming for me," she finally says breathlessly.

My muscles burn with fierce compulsion to haul her into my lap so I can hold her, give her solace until everything is better. Instead, I wait for the sign that it's okay to, my chest aching with the suppressed yearning to comfort. "I was coming for you. Was reaching the end of my rope when you appeared out of thin air today. You like doing that, I think, taking me by surprise. But the best one was today. I needed you the most today... this should be our reception." The last sentence falls out of my mouth before I can stop it.

Predictably, she looks out over the guests in front of her. "I would've helped you with whatever you needed, Blake. I wanted to, but you excluded me from some much, so I wasn't sure if you were going to want the baby. I couldn't bring myself to get an abortion. I thought there was nothing else left for me to do but quit my job and Arrow."

"And me. I'm glad you didn't get an abortion."

"And you," she says softly, regretfully. "Me too."

"I get why you ran though."

"You do?" Her head wrenches in my direction, staggered at my empathy, and that just isn't right. She should expect me to see her side of things. I'm a sheriff for God's sake. My job is to see everyone's perspective, even if I don't agree. Most times I don't, or I wouldn't need to be called in to referee a situation that's gotten completely out of hand by the time I arrive.

"Yes, I understand. I didn't give you a reason to stay, or encourage you to confide in me either. But your parents are good people and thank God they are. They took care of you when I couldn't."

"I do love my parents. They're just as understanding as you are and thought I was making rash decisions about…well, everything. Those mornings you saw me, my mother was trying to convince to tell you what was going on, but I wanted you too much, Blake. Can't think straight around you. I needed *you*. Too much, I think, not my parents, and needing would have erased my sound judgment." I'll never know how much it took for her to admit that, but I appreciate every effort it cost her.

"You can never need me too much, Astrid, and I should've been there." She didn't trust what we had enough to believe I would. "The next time you're feeling any type of way about *anything*, *talk* to me."

She clears her throat again, and nods. "So, what about your parents?"

The riblet turns to sawdust in my mouth. I set it back down gently on the plate. "They're snakes in couture clothing and expensive shoes that want me to give up the life I've made and take over theirs. I've given them a hard no once, but my father had a stroke three years ago and pleaded with me to leave the military and come back here so we could be a family. It was a ruse. He wanted me closer so he can work even harder on me, and I don't know what the right decision is to make concerning them, so I avoid them."

Astrid's features crumple up in her face.

Shit! She's mad.

125

"Blake, how blind can you be? You've already *decided*. You just don't want to hurt your parents with your decision. I can see your father now going on about his health and your mother looking pitiful behind him… or beside him. Wherever the hell she stands, manipulating people. It's a horrible thing to do to anyone, especially their son, and I'm sorry you're going through that."

Well, damn, she's right; I have decided, or I'd have taken the crown from my parents by now. I grab the napkin, destroying it by washing the BBQ sauce off.

"*We're* going through it, Astrid, and I'm sorry for the both of us. I guess you can say I'm legally blind when it comes to my folks, but it's much easier for you to see what's going on with us when you're standing on the outside looking in, isn't it?

She swallows. "That's where you wanted me to be."

"For good reason. The circle my blood family moves in doesn't take well to outsiders just like Pops said. Sure, you'll get invited into their homes to throw your money at their charities, but they don't ever really let anyone in unless you're Italian born or have wealth. You're more than enough for me just as you are. I don't know what I'd do if they hurt you for being *who* you are."

The situation hasn't even occurred yet, and anger is boiling within me. I take a swig from my wineglass, needing hard liquor to take the edge off, and sneak a look at Astrid. She's openly staring at me, with an amused look on her face. It draws me in. My pissiness diminishes.

"So you kept me on the outside because you didn't want them to reject me? As if I won't make them regret it."

"When you put it like that, it does seem like the dumbest move to make keeping you from them, but hell no I didn't want them to reject you. Why would I subject you to that, even if you have a rather damn smart mouth when you choose to use it?"

She tilts her head to the side in a silent 'touché' comeback then spears through a vegetable with her fork. "You got a point about your mother. She would *hate* me by the time I gave her a piece of my mind. What about the Owens? You didn't introduce me to them either."

"They would accept you... after some covert operations on Mama O's part."

Astrid starts to beat her neck with the soft side of her fist, as if there's food blocking her digestion. I thump her in the back lightly. Scientifically, it doesn't help a choking victim, but it's justification for... we all know what I'm doing.

Then she sips from her water glass. "Covert?"

"Yes, covert. Mama O's a former criminal with trust issues; she doesn't trust you until she's tried you. There are no limits to how she'll do it, and I thought your resemblance to Malisa would raise questions that she wouldn't hesitate to interrogate me about. She has a blank stare that's like looking into an abyss that looks back into you, until you give it what it wants. The truth!"

The deep, husky note of Astrid's laughter rings out. "I like this family. You did good finding a substitute for the creatures that hatched you, Blake."

Praise for me. Insults for my parents. That's a new level we've broken through, and we're pulling closer even if Astrid isn't aware of it yet. I revel in that, too.

"The Owens like you too, as you can tell. No one's interrupted our meal yet, probably because the Owens won't let them, and yes, my mother resembles a dragon. She dies her hair black and wears way too damn much makeup. I don't care if she likes you or not. You're mine. I'm yours. She can live with it or live without us. Her choice. Doesn't matter which she chooses. We'll be fine with or without any of the Powers. That's my promise to you and baby Blake, Astrid. If I ever break it, I better be breathing my last breath."

Her eyes close. Her hand twitches on the table. A single tear slips from the corner of her eye. She twists her face away from me. I know an emotional breakdown coming when I see one. Whether she wants me to console her or not, she needs it, and I'm going to provide it. She can cast me away afterwards.

"Come here, sweetheart." I lean towards her. She's already rotating around and raising her arms, dropping them on my shoulders and burying her nose in my neck. I cradle her in my arms. "I'm here for you, love, even when the sun stops shining, and the stars have fallen from the sky. You got me, and won't ever feel alone in anything."

Her fingers grip my hair as if she doesn't want to ever let go. Being permitted near her and having her look to me for support is an unexpected gift. Her red-hot blaze sears my throat and nose. Suddenly, I need a best man again.

I cart Astrid's chair closer instead, entomb my face in her hair until the feeling passes and she's not sniffling anymore. The sandwiched baby tumbles around inside her, kicking me in the abdomen as well as Astrid. Joy and awe bring the baking sensation right back in my nostrils.

"Shit!"

Nope, no formal wedding for me. I should be making the guests cry.

"Okay now, love?" I ask, sounding strangled.

She nods her head as she lifts her red-tinged orbs to my matching ones. "Sorry about that. You still get to me when nothing else does, and you found a new way to do it." With my words.

Thank God.

"That's a compliment, you know? And you can have a breakdown whenever you want to."

She sniffles and smacks me lightly on the chest. "You're not supposed to encourage a pregnant woman to cry, jackass." Name-calling now, just like my sister. Another level conquered.

Astrid's attention gets torn away by something behind me before the chinking of a glass being struck echoes over the prattle of the party. She sits back, her hand landing on my thigh.

"Apollo's about to steal your job," she informs, while looking over my shoulder.

I link her fingers with mine on my leg, clutching them, fully taking advantage of the moment. "Eat, Astrid. Everything may be closed when we leave and I don't want you going hungry before I can get you groceries in the morning."

"I—"

"Hmmm," I hum and incline my chin, cutting her off.

She rolls her eyes then rocks forward over her plate, with a small smile on her face. I pivot my head in the groom's direction, a giant over Malisa with her head canted up to him who's holding a microphone.

Please don't let this take all night, I pray to any heavenly being that's listening.

"If I can have everyone's attention. It's time for the best man's speech." He peeps down at his wife before returning his gaze to the crowd. "First, I'd like to thank Blake and Astrid for stepping in at the last minute to be bridesmaid and best man for us."

"I'd like to know why we got stuck with the penguin suits when there was supposed to be no wedding party!" I yell out, feeling more like myself, mischievous.

"Because I wanted you all dressed properly, ass hat," Malisa answers, giving everyone something to gurgle about. "Uncle Tommy would've worn his chef hat and apron. Uncle Luke would've stunk up the event with the smell of horse manure in his work clothes. You would've came in your sheriff's uniform, Blake."

"In other words, you didn't trust us," I shoot back, then stuff a riblet in my mouth.

"*Hell* no," she stresses with attitude and the roll of her neck.

Apollo sighs. "Blake, are you going to let me give the speech or what?"

"Or what," Tommy's voice stretches out from the middle of the setting, surrounded by the other Owens with a child in each lap, the oldest kids at tables bordering theirs. "That boy can't shut up when he drinks and won't talk when he's sober, a perfect example of Lydia's and Frank's backasswards raising."

"I'm sober, Unk!" I retort.

Pops slaps his forehead. "Shut up, Tommy, and let the man speak. Apollo, that is."

Uncle Tommy chucks, "You just want to eat, Frank."

"So do I, Tommy," Uncle Luke growls, "now shut the hell up… *please*."

"Natalia, his grumpiness is *your* fault," Uncle Tommy howls, must have the last word, although everyone he's talking to is sitting at the same table with him. "Feed and sex this man more often… *please*. It benefits us all."

His uncensored way of speaking causes Natalia to pitch wine down her chin then shrill with laughter. Astrid spits in her water that she's drinking, and puts it down quickly, then covers her mouth with her fist to keep the rest in.

I raise my hand. "Okay, enough of the Owens' antics. I got you, Apollo."

He bows to me. "Thank you, Sheriff. Now, the luckiest people on this earth are me, Blake, and now Astrid. The Owens go to bat for their own, whether blood related or not, and you better be up to par, or they'll boot your ass out."

"He cursed!" I holler out and jolt up in my seat. "And I couldn't? Oh, I know why!"

"Don't do it, Blake!" Malisa screams. "It's *his* wedding!"

"Oh, I'm doing it, sister!" I nod, vigorously, then laugh. "Just kidding. Go, Apollo. You got thirty seconds before the next interruption."

Somebody shouts twenty-nine. Uproars of hilarity follow.

Apollo heads spin around wildly. "Uh... Oh! The best day of my life was when Malisa started working for me and the best days haven't stopped coming since."

"That's because he's a reverse gold-digger," Malisa interrupts. "I run his damn company, keep his bank account flush, and then he tries to give me all the money. I'm a tax shelter. That's why he married me."

Apollo cracks up laughing along with everyone else then gapes down at her. "You too, huh?"

"Sorry, babe," she says with an unapologetic intonation in her voice that she isn't trying to conceal.

"You are so not sorry, my Lisa," he whispers into the microphone.

She smiles widely with her mouth slanted upwards. He bends to kiss it.

"Worse best man speech ever, Apollo" I goad. "You should've let me do it."

Apollo can't take his eyes from Malisa. "I rather kiss my wife anyway, Blake. Go for it."

I'd rather be kissing mine too, but showing and proving to Astrid that marrying me will never be an error will have to do for now.

"You weren't going to keep the floor long with this family around anyway," Uncle Luke barks out, then shovels food in his mouth.

Apollo extends the microphone to me with the sappiest of looks I've ever seen on his face for Malisa. I squeeze Astrid's hand before starting down the row towards him. Maria is kneeling behind the Malisa's chair, working at the tie in the net for the balloons while telling them off colorfully under her breath.

The woman is completely stressed and becoming unhinged.

When I take the microphone from Apollo's hand, he takes his place beside Malisa at the center of the table and resumes mashing faces with her.

"Congratulations to Mr. and Mrs. Apollo Nordic-Ford," I start. They look up finally, with their temples united and arms wrapped around each other. "Apollo, you already know you're a good man who deserves a wonderful woman like my sister. What you don't know is that no one here can be more proud of you than your father, who isn't able to be with us, but I'm sure he's here in spirit. Even heaven wouldn't have kept him from being a part of this day with you. You are also legally apart of the Owens now, and it is truly an honor to welcome you into the clan myself…

133

on paper. You were one of us when Malisa said she loved you with all of her heart."

Apollo nods with water-logged eyes.

I turn to the guests. "You did good, Sienna, even with the little time you had with your son before he was stolen away. The moment he was willing to face Mama O's black stare, we knew he was from good people too. If he wasn't, the Owens' influence would have surely made him the man he is today. This, I know for a fact."

Several sniffles let loose. Enough of that.

"*However*—" I begin again.

"Oh hell," Uncle Luke finishes.

"...the bro-code does not extend to patting a grown man on the back with tears in his eyes at his wedding. If it does, I'm making that rule obsolete right now. Do not *ever* ask me to be your best man, fellows, and I won't ask you to be mine." I spin toward Astrid sitting side saddle in her seat. "Because Apollo has already been drafted for the job of being my best man."

Astrid covers her mouth with both hands, her expanded irises visible even from where I stand. If there is truly a God in heaven, she will not be upset about the future proposal I'm promising her in front of an audience.

I grin at the groom. "Fair is fair, Apollo. I want my back patted every ten seconds at my wedding... gently, of course. Now, let's eat dammit! Thank you."

Lavender and white balloons rise. Maria plops down on her ass, kicks her shoes off, and rips a band from around the ball of her hair. She exhales.

Poor woman. I bet she's rethinking her profession after Apollo and Malisa.

Apollo raises up and pulls me into a bro-hug embrace then releases me, the ridges in my eyes a little moist.

I drop the mic on the table and walk off, with whistles, applause, and merriment tailing me back to my place beside Astrid, where I belong. Her wild-eyed expression hasn't changed.

I maneuver my chair sideways to face her before sitting down, then brush her elbow with my fingers.

"I'm sorry if I did I something wrong up there. I couldn't help myself. I promised myself I'd take it slow with you, and I messed up. Forgive me?"

She shakes her head and slopes toward me. I catch her with my arms, but she's really holding me. Massive amounts of relief dump in my system. Astrid jumps to her feet without letting me go, tacking her body over mine.

"Be careful, baby… of the baby," I caution.

More handclapping rivals the music now thumping through hidden speakers around the property. "We're being watched, sweetheart," I advise, while snuggling my cheek against her smooth, pale one.

She mumbles something against my neck. Eventually, I figure out she's saying, "Who gives two fucks?"

"Certainly not me."

I crook my finger beneath her chin to lift it, then recline my head back. Her lips collide into mine as if she's missing something and my mouth stole it. Violent clashes of our tongue result.

"Okay, lovebirds! Get a room," Malisa yelps, scandalized and delighted. "There's children present... and they're intrigued as hell as to what you two are doing over there!"

Pecking me on the mouth, Astrid reclaims her seat, her brow glued to mine. She's giggling, and damn if I'm not doing it along with her. Life is good. Finally.

The day slips by unnoticed as Astrid I concoct plans for merging our lives completely. She's coming back to Arrow, getting her old job back, but not her apartment. She will be moving into my mine tonight. It's bigger, two bedrooms, two baths, with open-plan living room and kitchen with a picture window that greets the sunrise every morning.

Amid stealing kisses and slow dances only possible after half the tables are stored away, it seems someone walks up and announces themselves to her every five seconds. A few are audacious enough to wax on, wax off baby Blake without permission. He kicks up a storm when they do it. We're not sure if he's pissy about it or happy because people are acknowledging him. My jeans begin to pulsate with an incoming call. I excavate the phone and greet Meagan, "Sheriff Powers."

"Blake," she says nervously. A bad sign. Meagan doesn't call me by my first name or do nervous at thirty-two-years-old and a former

Marine with respect for her superiors drummed into her. "I have Mr. Lindsey on the other line."

My hand begins kneading a groove into Astrid's spine. She sags into me, lining her chest with mine, thinking she's getting an unplanned massage when in actuality work is about to wrench me away from her, and I'm taking relaxation *from* her as fast as I'm giving it to her. "Meagan, not tonight please." I'm not above pleading.

Astrid's chin dips, hiding the scorching mask she wears when I'm going to get laid, possible all night. She cups her ear to the phone. "What's going on, Meagan?"

Meagan gasps. "Is that Astrid?"

"Yes," I say grittily, "and you're intruding, woman. What is it? Why didn't you call Copper?"

"Good to have you back, Astrid," rushes out of Meagan. "There's a bad wreck on the county line near the 195 marker, so Cooper can't leave until the scene is clear. Mr. Lindsey's on my home phone with the station's direct line forwarded to it. Lea's sick, and I have no babysitter. He's whispering into his cell that he's locked in the first-floor public restroom of his hotel. He's not being a nuisance this time, boss. There's two men ransacking the lobby, looking for a safe. I could hear them on the other side of the door talking loud like lunatics. Either they're out-of-towners who don't know there's no safe at Arrow's Renaissance, or they don't care that the hotel is open twenty-four hours with a staff. You have to check it out before they find him. There's no one else to do it but you."

Hiring more deputies becomes inevitable. I'm a family man now, except putting other people in harm's way and having to leave Astrid on our first night back together because I don't have a bigger work force leaves me gutted.

Damned if I do, damned if I don't.

Astrid nods, posture stiff, glare rigid; her deputy's guise. The blood in my veins swops with the kind of fear that makes bladders empty themselves prematurely.

"Oh hell no, you're not, Astrid. Don't even think about it. You are *not* going with me. You're staying here, where it's safe." My hands envelop her stomach. A meeting of the minds needed, I lay my forehead on hers. "When there's not two of you walking into danger, you can be my partner again. Deal?"

She exhales and pecks the end of my nose, wearing a sad expression that's tearing my heart out. "Be safe."

"Damn straight. I'll call when it's over and come back here so I can tail you home. Don't leave until I get back, baby. Promise me." Even my duties as an officer can't tear me away from her until she repeats the words, and it feels pretty damn good to call anything that's mine hers too.

"I promise," she says softly, pilfering one last caress from my lips before I jog off, slamming the phone to my ear on my way out of the gardens.

"On the way, Meagan. Three-way Mr. Lindsey for me."

"Will do, boss. Sorry about ruining your reunion with Astrid." Clicking, then ringing on her extra line reverberates in my earpiece.

"Reunion, huh?" I respond in the name of chit chat, while we wait for Mr. Lindsey to answer his second line. I couldn't care less if Meagan knows about Astrid and I, more interested in reuniting with her as soon as possible.

"Yes sir, boss, reunion. You two didn't fool anybody. Damn sure don't believe your 'rats in the station' lie. Copper and I have a bet on how long it'd be before you two got back together again. He lost. You're more stubborn than he thought." The ringing stops. "Mr. Lindsey, say something."

"Oorah," he rasps, a fellow Marine.

Military bonding. Great. "Should I yell out 'Hooah' since I was in the Army? Or can we talk about the situation at hand? Where did the burglars enter, Mr. Lindsey?"

"The front damn doors, while I was cleaning the restroom. I heard the bells on the door jingle and was just about to tell the customer I'd be out in a minute when I heard the side employee door to the front desk squeak. Someone yelled, 'Find the safe.' I locked the restroom real quiet like, so they couldn't get in, then called the sheriff's office direct. Thank AT&T for call forwarding. These guys are high on something too, or too stupid to know an operating hotel has a desk clerk somewhere in the building. Don't know which it is, don't care. I want them out, Sheriff Powers. Twenty years ago, you'd be scraping them off my sidewalk. If I get to my shotgun, you'll be wiping them off my walls."

Providing company for the burglars is the worst thing he can do.

"Don't leave the restroom to get your shotgun. You're pretty much safe where you are. Keep it that way. Can you hear them now? Where is your weapon?" The last thing I need is for them to find it. "Any guests or cleaners there right now?"

"Yes, I can hear the loud bastards. Weapon behind the counter, under the register, on the bottom shelf behind some extra towels. They probably have the gun by now though. No guests. Last one checked out this afternoon. Cleaners were gone by eight. The elevators and stairs access are locked down, lights off, so the little shits can't get farther than the first floor, and…" He trails off. I hope he's just listening for something and not preparing to defend himself.

"Mr. Lindsey," Meagan and I call out.

"I'm here," he whispers. "I think they've split up. It's quiet now, besides the rummaging going on behind the front desk. I'm guessing the other one's in the cooler or the laundry room, looking for only God knows what. Whoever's right outside the door at the desk is probably looking for the key to my register drawer since there's no safe that they keep talking about. The keys are on my wrist, stupid sons of turds!"

I don't know what's worse, a victim too scared to speak, or an ex-soldier too angry to stay quiet.

"Keep your voice down, Mr. Lindsey." If I keep him on the phone any longer, he'll draw the criminals right to him and probably lose his life.

"Meagan, keep him on your line, but no talking unless he thinks they're trying to get in the restroom with him. I'm at my truck and going to hang up now. Unless there's new developments on the scene before I get there, don't call me back. I'll radio Cara at dispatch on my way to the hotel."

"Got it, boss."

Chapter Nine

Blake

I heave the phone back in my pocket and my ass in the suburban, then flip the dash switches for the lights and sounds of the sirens. Sometimes, the noise is enough to clear out the perps. Anyone milling around afterwards is asking to be arrested. I tense up involuntarily. Not good.

These bastards are not going to go down easy.

My future wife and infant steal into my head as I pass by the spot on the road where they reentered my orbit this morning. Now, they're at the center of my world. Intending for them to stay there, I open the compartment beneath my elbow, relieve it of my handheld radio on the installed charger and my Glock 60, then lob the radio to my mouth.

"Cara, come in." I take a curve in the road almost too sharply. The back end of the truck bounces around. I slow down at an intersection seconds later.

Static from the two-way fills the interior of the truck with noise-reducing insulation. "Copy, Sheriff. What's your 20? I know where you're going already. Talked to Meagan. Copper will get there as fast as he can for backup."

"Old Arrow Road, heading east. Two minutes to destination."

"Be safe. Congratulations on Astrid coming back, Sheriff."

Seriously, Meagan!

Nothing secret in Arrow… ever.

"Thank you, Cara. Over and out until I have someone in custody… or not."

"10-4."

I sling the radio in the passenger's seat and veer right, the hotel six minutes away, well, sixty seconds at eighty-miles per hour. A green four-door, rusty Honda loiters under the extended roof of the hotel. Parking behind the car, I grab the radio, gun, and open the door.

"Cara, come in."

"Copy."

Flanked by the opened door and my truck, I peer into the glass walls of the hotel, looking for signs of movement at the front desk. It's quiet as death inside, and much more dangerous. "I'm on the scene. Run license plate Alpha Delta Brava 1093 out of Florida. Going behind enemy lines." The criminals own the building now.

"Check. Over and out."

After tossing the radio back in the truck, I retrieve my bullet vest from the back seat, strap it into place, clip the gun's safety off, and take aim.

"Sheriff's Department!" I yell at the doors while sweeping the car.

It's abandoned with fast food wrappers everywhere, along with used pipes for smoking dope. No way to tell how many junkies are hitting the place, but it's up to five at the max. The car couldn't possible hold more comfortably. Just three criminals looking for money is bad odds for me. I try hard to relax, or I'll shoot anything that moves. Mr. Lindsey better be still until this is over. That'll happen in a matter of seconds if it's up to me.

Astrid flashes in my mind. My neck bunches up to my ears. Tension climbs my spinal cord like it's a ladder. She's just more incentive to fire now, investigate who has my bullet in them later. I empty my thoughts then listen intently for noises that'll reveal the criminals' whereabouts, or where they headed. Nothing.

Too damn quiet.

Anticipation and adrenaline comingle. My trigger finger twitches. I fling one of the hotel's entrances wide with one hand, then wait for anything to pop off. Stillness reigns. I tread onto gold diamonds in red carpeting. The short end of the L-shaped foyer with burgundy couches and end tables backed against the walls is expectantly deserted. There's still the long end with the elevators and breakfast bar to clear.

The front desk is ransacked, with the employee gate folded up. Beside it is the iron barricade that Mr. Lindsey has secured from the other side. I point the business end of my Glock at the counter.

"Sheriff's Department! Raise your fucking hands slowly and come out even slower!"

I wait. If they're back there, then they're still back there. I ease up beside the antique register toppled over and check the floor littered with contents from the desks but no bodies.

Damn! Finding these fuckers is going to take a lot longer than I want it to.

I place my back to the restroom door, with my eyes trained on the cusp of the room. "Mr. Lindsey, are you okay?"

"No, I'm pissed!"

"You're in the right place then. Stay there until I tell you it's safe to come out."

"Whatever!"

Such a crabby old man. Pushing off the bathroom's door, I skulk toward the long end of the lobby. "Sheriff's Department! Come out with your hands up goddamnit!" Nada.

Fine, we'll do it the hard way then.

I drift toward the short span of wall, stop at the corner, and glimpse around the upturned chairs on the tables and the halogen-lit alcove for the breakfast bar at the rear. Ceiling-to-floor windows swamp the room with dying sunlight that's rebounding off the surface of the closed doors on the opposite side. Shoulder against cream-painted edge of the wall, I swing around the corner and try the first door.

After spinning the knob, I kick it, to cause damage to whatever's behind it. No one screams out that their nose or ribs is broken, but they're still trapped, even if they're slim enough to avoid my preemptive strike.

I eyeball the space behind the hinges. It's vacant. Perps still loose in the building. An industrial-size washer and dryer yawn at me from across the room. The gap between us is full of bath products and silver rectangles that scattered when someone collapsed a steel rack and ripped the legs off it. Weapons for perps, check.

I slink to the next door. It swings wide. A person in a black hoodie overcasting their face charges at me with an iron bar raised above their head.

"Stop and drop it!"

They don't, but it's a man, my height. Astrid flits through my mind, and I am going home to her, so I squeeze the trigger. He buckles at the waist.

"You killed him!" someone shouts manically from behind me before perp number one hits the ground on his side.

I do a one-eighty then yell the same command that the first criminal ignored. Similarly dressed perp number two doesn't obey either. He's wielding a raised crowbar. I fire. Perp number two with a hood gets blown backwards. Bow-legs in too damn big, dark work pants that are attached to suspenders shuffle into my line of sight. Ready to bust another cap in somebody else's ass, I recognize Mr. Lindsey's customary ensemble that the 80's want back. A shotgun is lined up with the creases of his pants.

"Dammit, old man! I told you not to come out or get the gun! Now, go back! There could be more!"

Then something blacks out my peripheral view. I glance over and sidestep simultaneously toward Mr. Lindsey, the hardhead who needs his ass covered.

"Duck, Sheriff!" erupts from him suddenly as he raises the 12-gauge and pumps it.

Something slams into the top of my head first. Mr. Lindsey's weapon breaks the sound barrier as I sink under the vicious blow, eardrums buzzing. Everything goes dark.

****

"You can't sleep with a head injury, Blake. You've got to wake up. Right now!" The abrasive command is punctuated with the shaking of my shoulders.

"Stop," I demand groggily, then roll over to my back and groan. There's a heavy metal band playing in the room, and they have no talent whatsoever, or one hell of a migraine is coming on. No recollection of ever having those before comes to mind. So why am I about to suffer one now?

"God, what happened to me? Where am I?"

"Blake, don't move," comes from above me. "You've been clobbered by a damn burglar. We took him and his heathen comrades down though. They're all dead. I checked. I told that council of yours that we needed a regular patrol out here at night. Just sit still, and I'll bring you something back for the bleeding and call Deputy Daniels."

My council? Deputy Daniels! Whoever that is. Who is this man talking to me?

I squint up at him then mash my fingers to my temple. "Do I know you?" Warm liquid flows throw my fingers from a slit in the goose egg forming on my scalp. It throbs under my probing.

An old man's grizzled-up face wrinkles even more, distress sitting heavily on the age lines. "You've known me just about all your life, Blake. I'm Mr. Lindsey."

"That is a negative… Mr. Lindsey."

"Shit! Tell me you remember me, at least Deputy Daniels and what you're doing here, or that you don't have amnesia."

Try as I might to honor just one of his requests, disorientation is the ruler of my existence right now. "I can't tell you anything about… any of that," I confess, and sit up amongst other people asleep in the oddest of positions with black hoods over their heads.

Blood pools beneath all of them, soaking into the rug. Too much to still be alive. They're dead. I don't panic like a normal human would, which is disturbing. I point at the closest one.

"Is that what I was doing here?"

He drops the butt of a shotgun on the ground and huffs, "Yes, you're the sheriff. I was being robbed. You came here alone, off-duty."

Apparently, that was a serious mistake.

But where I came from seems less significant than the cannon standing beside him and the unknown reason for the bulletproof vest on my chest. I pat it with both hands.

Yep, definitely something an officer who likes living would own.

"Well, if I'm the cop, why do you have the gun?"

"This is mine. Good thing, too. I shot the one who knocked you senseless with an iron leg, or he'd have probably killed you with it. Your gun is behind you."

I rotate around at the waist. Sure enough, there's a firearm behind me. I pick up it and examine it in the palm of my hand. The weight feels familiar.

"I'm the sheriff." I say skeptically, searching my memory banks for evidence of that, coming up with blank spaces and fuzzy images of people at a party, lavish affair held in a mansion a mile back from the road behind a wrought-iron fence. Not an affair I'd attend if I could get around it.

"What's your full name, Blake?"

I explore my gray matter for that answer, too. Well, I know what my brain is made of, so my education is still intact. But whose name went at the top of my school work? The image of a slender, blond man in a suit, and dark-haired lady who's as skinny as a rail in a green, sequined dress materialize. They surely aren't my name, which I guess is Blake. But the people in my head might know for sure, I think. I'll ask them. Except, I don't know where they are.

The strong propulsion to fondle my jaw drives my hand up to do it. Must be a worry-reflex because it keeps me from losing my shit.

"Well, I'm going to assume my first name is Blake, because you keep calling me that, but as for the rest of my names… if you find out before I do, let me know."

The old man's shoulders depress. His freckled bald head encased in wire-rimmed glasses rolls heavenward. "Well hell! I should've come out sooner. Just sit. I don't want you falling down if you get up, and I'll make sure an ambulance gets here on the double, or they'll hear from me and my lawyer."

I prop back on my hands, while wishing the headache away.

The old man limps around a turn and croaks loudly, "Deputy Miles! Jesus Christ, thank you for getting here. Blake took a blow to the head and his memories leaked out of his scalp."

"What?" A deep tone with authority behind it responds.

I get an image of a tan shirt, brown slacks, wide shoulders, and three little brown-haired kids, two boys and one girl who look like no one I've ever seen before. Of course, I can't remember who I've seen, so that doesn't count for much. A bodybuilder with hair color identical to the kids lumbers toward me with his thumbs hooked in his utility belt. I visualize a church with a big, red X on it. Now, that is plenty weird.

He wobbles his head, hair tapered on the sides, super short strands on top styled to lay in every which way on purpose. "Damn, boss, what happened?"

Boss. Not awkward. Must be true. "Don't have a clue. Deputy Miles, right?"

He extends a hand to me, his ever-present humor written in the shallow laugh lines around his mouth. I don't think twice about accepting his aid up, which almost dislocates my shoulder from the socket. I don't even blink. Rough must be our way of doing things.

On my feet, my head spins. A pregnant woman in a white, sleeveless dress, satiny caramel skin, tight curls, and delicate hands pops up behind my eyes. Jasmine outbreaks in the lining of my nose. I forget to inhale.

All normal reactions to her, Blake, trespasses through my psyche.

So, who is she? Wondering makes my head ache more, so I stop, straighten my clothes. Maybe, she'll show up too and tell me who she is herself.

Copper balances his weight on outstretched black boots. "You guessed right, boss. Deputy Copper Miles at your service. I got an ambulance and the coroner on the way. Can you believe he's excited to be working a crime scene with actual bodies that didn't die a natural death?"

My eyebrows shoot up. "Is this town *that* sleepy?"

He grins, stark-white teeth bright enough to make my eyes hurts, no, they were paining me anyway.

"We *were* that sleepy until crime started picking up about a year ago. Stolen cars. Break-ins. I assume these three here are the reason why. Their ride was stolen out of Florida a month ago. I think they've been laying low here for quite a while. They should've picked someone else's town instead of yours."

Mine's. No, not strange either.

The radio on his shoulder blares to life. "Copper, come in. Don't say anything else to the boss. Dr. Ellis said telling him what he doesn't know, even accidentally, could hurt his chances to recover his memory. He must fill in the blanks himself. Ambulance's ETA is less than thirty seconds. God, this is so sad."

Copper frowns and pulverizes the transmit button on his radio with his thumb. "Copy that, Cara." He cups my elbow. "Come on, bo… ah, just come on. We're contaminating the crime scene and need to wait for the ambulance at your… outside the lobby of the hotel."

The paramedics arrive as we exit the foyer. A white suburban idles behind a beat to hell, four-door sedan.

Enemies' car, probably.

Pacing by the hood of it is Mr. Lindsey, with his hands cradling his phone. I imagine he would pace, since his place of business will be roped off with yellow tape for a while and he won't be allowed anywhere near it. Him living somewhere else other than the hotel doesn't fit though, so this is probably his only home, which means he'll be out of one for the time being.

Astrid

Fifteen miles away

With my feet glued to the very spot Blake left me in, I witness the adoration and love oscillating around Malisa and Apollo as they sway to the bass line of Tatyana's "Do Not Disturb," a sensual tune with hedonic lines that have me pining for Blake already. It's almost like I'm infiltrating a private moment belonging to only the bride and groom who are completely lost in each other. A smile forms on my mouth. If they weren't tuning out the family and friends on their special day, I'd be concerned.

May real life be busy elsewhere, at least until this day is done for them.

They've earned the portion of heaven they've transported to in each other's arms, after showing a complete stranger kindness, with no idea if they can trust me or not. That reminds me, I haven't talked to the people who do know me through and through, my family.

My mother will be more than glad to sidetrack me with questions about everything that happened today while Blake's gone. As much as I want to go with him, enforcing the law is no place for baby Blake. Not wanting to leave the reception without letting someone know where I'll be, I caress Malisa's bare shoulder to divert her attention but only for a second. With a dreamy countenance, her head wheels to me.

"I'll intrude just a minute, you two," I say quickly. "I'm going in the house to call my parents and let them know I won't be back to

153

Harrison. I'll return the pantsuit after I get it cleaned, Malisa. Be right back."

God willing, so will Blake.

Malisa hugs me tight before I can make like a tree and leave them alone again in their own universe. "The pantsuit and shoes are my gift to you to welcome you and baby Blake into the family."

"I should be getting you a gift."

She embraces me a little tighter. "You did, Astrid. A nephew, Blake's happiness, and someone for me to call sister are what you gave me. Nothing in this world can top that. Tell your parents we all said hello and they're welcome to come up anytime. There's more than enough guestrooms at the castle for them and you too."

A castle is appropriate for her and Apollo's love story. It's the stuff that fairytales are made of, and I'm keeping them from theirs a lot longer than I want to.

"Okay, Malisa, I'm accepting the outfit but only this time because I'm intruding, and thank you. I'll pass your message on to my parents who would love to visit."

I kiss her cheek. Apollo takes her back in his arms. Heaven for them recommences as if I never interrupted. Inside the house, I find my belongings where I left them, on Luke's and Natalia's chest of drawers beside their bed. The iPhone reclines face up on the sack stuffed with the presents from Malisa. It rings before I can pick it up.

The number and name displaying hasn't graced my screen in months. Shouldn't be doing it now, because I'm not an officer anymore.

What would he have to call me about now?

My scalp prickles.

Blake!

Numbness sets in as I swipe the accept-call icon. "Mr. Lindsey, where's Blake?"

"Something happened," he replies with angst.

My chest shatters outward. Ethereal ragged ends of my skin flap against my breasts. My fingernails grapple at them, trying to fix the damage done just so I can breathe, but you can't repair what's doesn't really exist. Mindset blown wide open, I start to hyperventilate.

He's not dead. He's not dead. Dammit, he's not dead!

The chant repeats as the four chambers of my heart shrink, rebuffing functioning, withholding blood to my brain.

"Deputy Daniels, I know you'd want to know if something like this happened, as close as you and Blake are. They hit him from the blind side but the ambulance is here seeing about him. He's fine. Physically anyway." Ringing in my ears drowns out his coarse, low-pitched voice.

I scuffle to make sense of his words.

"Wait. What? He's fine?" But if Blake is alright, why does Mr. Lindsey sound like someone just burned his precious hotel down to the ground?

Because everything isn't fine, and you know there are things worse than death.

Mr. Lindsey doesn't answer, denying me relief. My knees crumble. Fingers clench at the dresser's brim. I use it to lower myself to the floor, then spread my feet as wide as I can, and dunk my head as low as the baby bulge will let me. Deep breaths don't result. Heart won't stop pounding. Intuition won't stop baying.

I should feel better by now, but I know something worse is coming. It'll kill me to recover from the trauma I'm experiencing then be notified that Blake won't make it through his ordeal, so I'm left with an unending state of perpetual anxiety. Yet, I prepare… For what, I don't want to know, but can't dodge the truth. It's like a horrific accident that you can't look away as it happens, horrified, yet, stuck in the moment, eyes wide, pulse thumping, unable to do anything but witness.

"What's wrong with Blake, Mr. Lindsey?" I ask through chattering teeth.

"Deputy Daniels, honey, breathe." That's impossible right now.

"Spit… it… out… Mr. Lindsey."

"He was attacked and has a bump on the noggin, and…" The sudden lull in his description of Blake's accident is like enduring nails scraping a chalkboard.

"And!"

"Amnesia," comes gently from him but bears down on me like a hurricane.

I gasp then explode up, bashing the wood with my back as if it's to blame for Blake's cerebral reboot. Spine against the dresser, elbows stabbing my knees, and fingertips clawing at my ears, I scramble to make my lungs work. "No, no, no, I just got him back."

"I know, Deputy Daniels." How does he know too?

Who cares how he knows? Blake's gone again, but I don't really know that, do I?

"Does he remember me?" I wheeze, my sanity dangling from a mantle made of faith that's such a fragile thing. If I'm correct, I only need a mustard seed's worth. Sheer determination to believe in a miracle preserves me from going off the deep end.

"Deputy Daniels, honey—"

"Say it, Mr. Lindsey."

"Maybe you should wait for—"

"Say it!" I start to rock back and forth, knowing the answer. The mustard seed withers, my resolve to retain my lucidity by any means necessary losing traction.

"It's, Deputy Daniels, I don't think—"

"SAY IT!" I scream.

Baby Blake startles inside me.

"No, Deputy Daniels … he doesn't remember you."

There being something worse than death is confirmed.

"I asked him if he did, Deputy Daniels. I knew you two were dating. Anyone that saw you two together could tell."

My vison coils up and shrivels to nothing. I'd loved to follow in its footsteps, but I can't. No one outside helping Malisa and Apollo celebrate has any idea of the tragedy that's looming over them. The weight of it will crush the Owens, who'll cinch on to the nearest family member just to stay vertical. Everyone will fall, ruining Malisa's and Apollo's day. I don't want that for them, or to be the bearer of this bad news.

"Stay on the phone, Mr. Lindsey."

"Okay."

I flip over to my knees, then stumble to my feet, staggering to the door as if I drank everything at the bar.

Chapter Ten

Astrid

Disjointed thoughts and incomplete sentences slash through my head. Luck with love, fucked up. Or shitty. Has to be piss-poor at least. Can't decide which, after getting the man I want in just the way I want him, and now goddamn amnesia has him pinned down. Out of commission. My world going to hell twice. Broken again. When do the hits stop coming? Kicking me and the baby when we're down. Punching us. Over and over.

"Astrid!" Malisa shrieks beside me, from the middle of the backseat of Apollo's navigator, her hand gripping mine way too tightly.

"What?" I answer dejectedly with head hanging low, shoulder saddling the back-passenger window that's helping me stay erect to some extent.

She should be in the front seat with Apollo, who's not driving fast enough but going too fast. I don't want to see Blake, but I wish I had wings. I'll already be at the hospital, cowering in the hallway. I don't want to see the unfamiliarity in Blake that I'll surely get when I walk into his sight. Then I'll have to go home with my tail tucked between my legs, a loser in love again.

Apollo keeps one eye on the road, one on his wife in the rearview mirror.

I'm coming between them again with my problems.

Although it's Malisa who wants to sit back here with me, I don't need the company.

The other Owens trail us in their cars, reception cancelled an hour and a half before time for Malisa and Apollo to take their leave. Fairytale put off indefinitely. So damn messed up. Someone should have a happily ever after. Apollo and Malisa get my vote.

Her hand stuffs the hair falling in my face behind my ear. "No time for this woe-is-me crap, sister. Our boy has lost his mind, literally. He needs it back before the Powers get their hooks into him, and only you can help him get it back. You and baby Blake, so get your shit together. Stop with the pity party, and come up with a plan before his parents get to the hospital. You're the damn cop here. Do something." Malisa is warrior. Me, limp noodle.

"Ex-cop." I regret giving up my badge now. It could be used in the place of blood ties and the marriage license that I don't have. We'll all need it to get past the hospital personnel. Instead, I only have future fiancé status, which means nothing to everyone but me.

Air swishes out of Malisa's mouth, adding more warmth to my heated cheeks. "Whether ex or not, cop is attached, Astrid. Good enough for me. Now, do your ex-job. Think!"

"I can't slap him with a warrant for his memories and make him give them up. I don't have a badge to do it if I could. We can't even tell him who he is without risking planting memories that aren't real and blocking the real ones from coming back." Which means he doesn't even recall he pledged to ask me to marry me.

But oh, how I wanted it to happen.

Got this close to it, needed it. Need him still, which is just another blow, reaming what's left of my strength out of me.

"Him remembering us is the least our problems, Astrid," she spits.

Does she know how absurd she sounds? Suddenly, irrationally furious, I whirl around on her like I'm possessed because I am, with desolation which lashes out at everyone.

"What could be worse than him never remembering me, Malisa? Huh? Tell me, please! Even him being dead fails to trump love and baby forgotten."

And Malisa can't see that because she's not in love with Blake, idiot.

Shit. Taking my despair out on the wrong person.

She rears back into her father's bulk, eyes the size of soccer balls, then points her finger in my face and recoups the space she retreated from. "Don't go psycho ex-cop on me! Ashley and Martin are *worse*. They'll use this to their advantage. They're low enough to *plant* memories in his head, Astrid. We'll all lose Blake for good. We have to make sure he comes home with us and you… tonight."

Oh God, forgot about his parents. I'm suddenly exhausted again. Slumping now. "Sorry, Malisa, about taking my problems out on you, but it isn't Apollo who's forgotten you, so you can't understand. I pray you never have to. Trust me, Sienna will be the least of your worries."

I use the webbing in my thumb and index finger to almost gouge my eyes out of my head. They're extremely dry and spasm like the devil, which gets even more hellish every time Malisa conjures up an idea that won't work.

"Listen to me, Malisa. I'm not married to him. We're not even properly engaged, so his parents legally get first shot at being his guardians if the doctor says he needs one until he remembers who he is. It doesn't matter who *we* are… all because Ashley regurgitated him like the snake she is." I bet Martin has a tiny prick too.

"So what now?" she asks, disappointed almost as much as I am.

"Unless Blake chooses to come home with one of us, and I don't have a home here anymore by the way, can't lawfully enter his without him, we're stuck trying to get past the Powers with the law on their side to get to him. I don't think we have a snowball's chance in hell of getting past either one. His amnesia plays right into their hands and we're out."

"Astrid, you have a home as long as I'm alive, and *we* can prove they're unfit parents. They were never there for him as a child."

I know where this is going. Court. Nope. Ruining what's left of hers and Apollo's honeymoon time before the babies arrived by crashing at their home. Uh huh. Excruciating eyeball pang. Present. "He's not a child, and they haven't done anything abusive or harmful yet to warrant the law's intervention."

I could check on him if I had the Arrow Sheriff Department behind me though. No, wait. Eight months pregnant. One month and six weeks of maternity leave before I can wedge a way into his life legally. Time is a massive elephant and effective blockade. Blake is lost to me and baby until then.

"Astrid, them talking him into doing something to himself that he never wanted should be criminal. So should cutting us out of his life and working for their snobby ass companies with snobby ass board members instead of letting him be around the ones who love him the most."

"It hasn't happened yet, and there's no history of them hurting him as a child or adult. We're screwed royally." No KY jelly. No warning of what's coming from behind. No Blake in my future.

"Calm down, ladies," Apollo's deep, gloomy tenor drums into my spiraling thoughts. "Both of you have babies on board and we want them to stay that way. We'll figure out something together, even if it's praying morning, noon, and night that his memory comes back as soon as possible... like in the next few minutes."

Too long. Need him now.

"I know, Astrid. Damn, I know," Malisa murmurs, then swirls me around in the seat by the shoulders and dumps me in her arms, or she tries to.

My head is laying topside in her chest. I'm hunched over her babies, getting two nostrils full of her dress, and thinking out loud now. Losing it. Big time.

Get it together then. Slap yourself or something.

No energy.

Ask someone else to do it.

Hurting enough already.

Then do it for his baby.

Nothing I can do apart from wait. More damn waiting. Never gets me anywhere when it comes to Blake.

Exactly!

Need to be with him. Touch him. Let him see me.

That might work for you both, you know?

Only option left. Got to man up... no, woman up now. Except my idea of rallying is to encircle Malisa's torso with my arms, stealing her will to fight by touch, while she shushes me and strokes my back.

Frank snickers to himself and reaches over the front passenger seat, touching Lydia's shoulders. "Yep, these two could be sisters. Arguing one minute, then holding onto each other for dear life the next. We'll get in Blake's room if I have to throw my weight around, girls. *All* of it."

Funny. Frank would hurt someone. I would laugh at his joke but that would take too much exertion. I reach for his other hand, palms down, on the seat beside Malisa. I can't take too much of her strength. She's pregnant three times over and needs her essence just to stand. Frank seems to have plenty grit to go around though. His fingers curl around mine, willing to share. Owens and Nordic-Fords, the best.

"Yes, we are, sweetheart, because we're there for one another," Lydia murmurs. "And we got you."

Lydia reaches between the seats, to draw circles in my lower back, which is growing stronger by the minute. Arrow General Hospital springs up in Frank's window like a phoenix. The three-level structure resemble a bird. The east and west wings are shaped like Plexiglas triangles spreading out from the top floor. Humongous, neon-red 'A' centered on the roof like a cone-shaped head.

Ugliest construction I've ever seen, but an extraordinary example of what I should be doing; rising to the challenge. If an architect can get paid for sketching that building, which is lending me hope when I can't find on my own, then I can do what needs to be done to save Blake from his own flesh and blood. I could do better, if I could throw my weight around like Frank, too. Stomp the Powers even, if I had money and power like the owner of this hospital has, or even had been on the council that approves city projects like... the hospital. An idea begins to take shape.

The cell phone suffocating in my fist becomes a lifeline.

****

Blake

It's probably rude to mean-mug the bulletproof vest that's flopping off a chair in my emergency room fashioned from a sheet hung from a circular rod, while the doctor is trying to diagnose me, with lots and lots of questions. Yet, I'm doing it, because it isn't a vest I needed when I went to Mr. Lindsey's hotel.

I needed a damn helmet.

Now, I've disremembered... Is that a word? I do believe so. At least, I'm not stupefied about who I am anymore. Whatever narcotic is in my system has locked down the pessimism that was rapidly approaching but not the hollowness in my core as I endured the MRI scan. I don't need to know who I am to decide that feeling just shouldn't be there, and why it is. Something and someone essential to my existence have been misplaced. I mean to locate each missing piece until I'm whole again.

The chart in Dr. Ellis' hand slaps the side of the bed, snapping my attention to him. He folds his thick arms across his even thicker chest and furrows his pale brow already marred with crinkles.

He does not get outside much.

"Mr. Powers, are you listening to me?"

"Yes," I deadpan. But not really.

A low murmuring picks up in the hall, along with the collective outline of a group yielding shadows on the white, thin cotton walls of my makeshift room behind the doctor's back.

"Same rule applies. Only two at a time," a female says coldly. "Wait here."

A figure breaks away from the group, punches through the flimsy partition of my room. Blue scrubs pour in behind Dr. Ellis. Wearing them is a plump woman, with an olive skin tone and her mouth compressed. She doesn't have to open it for me to know she's the one who laid down the law, lives by the book, and has some sort of lead position here. "Doctor, there's a call for you and it's urgent."

He whirls around. "Fine, Sasha. Be right back, Mr. Powers."

"That chick is mad, Frank," a tinkling voice full of amusement chirps as Dr. Ellis and the nurse leaves.

Being popped on the back of the head from a stern hand for misbehaving is all I can think of.

"Of course, she is, Lydia. We went over her head, baby, and she had to let us back here anyway," a profoundly rough, equally amused tone replies. "I think I like having clout. You two go first."

Another man being popped in the back of *his* head comes to mind. I assume it's the same person doing the popping.

A dark chocolate hand hammers the slit in the sheet, nudging it apart. A woman trudges through it in a white dress, satiny caramel skin, and tight curls, needing the wafer-thin mattress much more than I do to stabilize the massive girth in front of her. She's the woman I had the vision of at the hotel, but her dress is different, and the physical response I had doesn't fire off.

She's not mine.

Never was or we've both clearly moved on. That doesn't stop me from growing apprehensive about her pregnancy throwing her off balance at any moment. I care for her apparently, and there has to be at least three babies in her. Her attire is a bit odd for a hospital visit though. The first thing I want to do is tease her about it.

"Is that a wedding dress?" I ask.

A big grin snakes across her lips as she bobs her head for a response. She's as cute as a button, her belly outweighing the rest of her body. I throw my legs over the side of the bed then freeze.

Good Lord, tell me I didn't marry this woman before getting my head split to the white meat.

Despite my alarm, I pat the mattress beneath me. "Congratulations. Come sit down here. I'll get up."

Before she gets to my bedside, Dr. Ellis comes back in a clipboard swinging, sulky mood. "Stop."

She does. He swerves around her, bends down, and slings my ankles right back where they were on the bed, ticking me off.

"Man, she's pregnant! Let her sit down comfortably!" If he doesn't, there's going to be a problem.

"No," he fires back, then grabs the blanket bunched at the bottom of my feet, straightens it out, and then chucks it over my legs as if that's all he needs to immobilize me. "She can sit in the chair with the vest unless she needs a much more comfortable chair brought in here. You're on strong sedatives and need to *lay* down until I discharge you tomorrow, Mr.

Powers. I'm tempted to put her in her own room though. There has to be at least three babies in her." He begins scribbling on his paperwork.

I snort and grumble, "That's what I think too. I'm surprised she can walk."

She giggles. "I can hear you, you jackass." I laugh at her nonvenomous slur. She probably aims several of those at me every time we're in the same vicinity, so I must know her, or she wouldn't be here. Right?

I'm laughing when another woman in the actual white dress that I envisioned, satiny caramel skin, and tight curls toddles through the hole in the linen much less pregnant than the last woman, with a phone to her ear. Her solemn expression is targeting the ground. My hilarity dies in my throat.

There's two of them! Both pregnant! Can't be, unless their twins. Ummm, no that doesn't fit. But what does?

I start to doubt my own rationality.

My eyes canter to the woman who's removing the vest from the chair to nestle it on top of the possible triplets she carries, then my gaping swerves back to the woman talking low into the receiver.

She stops at the foot of the bed, staring down at my feet. She places a hand on the footboard, nails digging trenches in the hard plaster. She's strung tight, and all I want to do is make it better… and get my hands on her belly.

Too far, Blake, my good manners yap, but my instincts don't think so.

Evidently, they're not afraid of not being politically correct all the time.

"Okay... Okay... I'll see you at the station in the morning, and thank you for doing this for us, again. Have a good night." She hangs up the phone. Creamy honey orbs touch down on my face. They're a little too creamy. What is making her want to cry?

"Hi," she speaks softly, with a trace of relief in her cadence.

The muscles in my jaw go flaccid, lungs seize up. Just quit working. *She's* the pregnant woman I imagined at the hotel. My nerve endings grow raw, reacting to her mere presence.

"Hi."

Touch her now, rockets through my head, and I will, as soon as she says it's fine with her.

Her lips open and close, like there's something she wants, no, needs to say. While I wait for her to get up the nerve, slanting my mouth against hers becomes an obsession.

God, I hope I had sense enough to sleep with this woman at least once... a day.

What if she isn't mine? If she was, she's undeniably met someone else since she's pregnant... eight months along, I suspect. I think I'd remember if I had a baby on the way. Hatred for the other man injects itself into my veins, which constrict in my neck.

The woman in the chair with the sun sparking from her face turns glum. "He really doesn't know who we are, Astrid."

Astrid. Beautiful name. Even more beautiful woman. Her, I'll marry right now, with the egotistical nurse and too-talkative doctor as witnesses. Stirrings in my groin produce a tent in the blanket. I lock my hands together over it but can't help staring at Astrid. It all feels quite routine, truthfully.

Astrid drops her head again. "We expected this, remember, Malisa?"

"Jasmine," I say the first thing that comes to mind. Anything that'll get her eyes back on me will do.

She covers her face with both hands instead. I didn't want her to finish her descent into crying though.

"I'm sorry," immediately breaks through my teeth.

They're clamping together, hands clenching, and I want to go to her to put them all on her, calm her down. It'll work. I'm positive of it. Her neck whips up, finally. She nods, rims of her eyes wholly wet.

"Don't be sorry, Blake. That's my favorite perfume." Then she half-smiles. Much better, somewhat. I rather be exposed to her full grin.

Two shadows materialize on the strung-up sheet, abducting my awareness that wants to be concentrated only on Astrid.

"Dr. Owens and Lydia," emits from the new guests.

It's like they're parrots. Two people return the greeting with a lukewarm impersonation. Common sense says it's Dr. Owens and Lydia speaking, and one of them has a mean open palm. I memorize the quality of their voices, which I can almost guarantee gets much warmer than lukewarm.

A man and woman breeze in the soft entrance as if they belong here, with a frigid flair haunting their slender frames, and bored vibes. I guess they should be here since they look like the people I thought of right after I couldn't figure out my name, which my parents surely would have given me. Yet, I'm not all that thrilled to get reacquainted with them. Mothers and fathers aren't supposed to look like mannequins when their offspring is in the hospital. Or maybe it's just mine who are like this, and they make a total of four visitors.

Sasha is going to have a meltdown, and hopefully asks them to leave on the double.

The thought has barely been established when she spanks the sheet from the outside, a hand propping on her hip.

"Ma'am and sir," she says icily, "there're too many people in here. Two of you will have to leave. So many people will aggravate his condition."

My parents' backs congeal as if someone is hosing them down from behind.

"I'm his mother." Her reply and bearing isn't any warmer than the nurse's, and it doesn't feel off about her, when it should. "This is his father. We're Ashley and Martin Powers, so make the *others* leave... *ma'am.*"

Astrid tenses up as her head whirls to Malisa, who growls quietly. I see that she's protective of me. Heart of a lion and a sister. I like that very much.

Dr. Ellis shakes his head. "They're fine, Sasha. That's what the call was about. Stay for a minute. Mrs. Powers, Blake has post-traumatic amnesia. He was hit hard enough to cause a lesion on the part of his brain called the hippocampus. It's responsible for the encoding, storage, and retrieving of memories. Naturally, after this tragedy, those functions were disrupted. It's as if the burglar knew exactly where to land the blow at on top of Blake's head to affect that part of his brain. Blake's pre-existing memories are gone."

Astrid levels her head against the heel of her hand, elbow resting on the crown of her tummy. Pure grief fluctuates from her, but she keeps her composure and doesn't reach for me like I want… I should say I long for her to, while my mother palms her freckled chest that's burdened with several strings of pearls. She seems genuinely floored, and I debate if I was wrong about her. Then her blues eyes hone in on my father's browns. They share a mutual uplift in their demeanor, which rounds out their stark bird-like features that could do with an extra ten pounds.

They quickly cover up their soundless discussion and strange moment of happiness with matching thunderstruck disguises once again. Predators are what they are, too busy preying instead of eating, which most likely consists of a liquid diet of the alcoholic variety. I wouldn't find it incredible if they can transfer thoughts to one another. Reading each other well and having the same agenda is what births power couples. These two can be considered that, and I should stay far away from them, if I listen to my intuition banging around my middle section.

"Is he going to be okay?" they ask together with a convincing display of dread interwoven around their words. They would've gotten away with their exhibition, if I hadn't been studying them both closely.

"In time, but I have to insist that no one divulges facts of your lives with Blake around him. He needs to come to them on his own if he's to get his accurate memories back." Dr. Ellis barely diverts his attention in Sasha's direction, but I catch it.

Her hand slips from its perch on her ample hip, and she pivots on the heels of her black clogs to hoof it out of here, uttering, "Someone knows some pretty powerful people to be breaking the hospital rules for one man."

Really? Who would wield the influence of the powerful to get to me? Surely not my parents who wouldn't need it since they're my kin. Astrid then? If only I was so lucky.

The doctor's head cants to her then Malisa. "So you two aren't his family?" I get the notion that he is going somewhere with his inquiry.

"Of course not!" my mother screeches under the black hairdo that is washing out her scaly skin and amplifying the crow's feet around her blue eyes, refusing to be veiled by her makeup. Dragon lady, I mean my mother, gives the women the once-over, stopping on Astrid. "Do I know you?"

The temperature drops. I sit up, on edge and ready to defend Astrid *and* Malisa.

"No, you don't... but you will," Astrid comments, then turns sideways, widespread fingers scaling each side of her stomach.

My palms itch to be flat against the backs of her hands, and there's no limit to the things I'd do for that to be my child in her.

174

"Hello, Mrs. and Mr. Powers." Malisa executes a parade wave, with her middle digit more stiff than the other ones that are just bent enough to raise a valid dispute of whether she is or isn't shooting a bird at my parents.

I already know which is accurate and conclude that Astrid and Malisa don't need defending by me or anyone else. I cough into my hand, concealing my grin.

My mother harrumphs and knocks invisible wrinkles out her dress, which is red, short sleeves, knee-length, and enhances her 'dragon lady' appeal. I expect her to start breathing fire at any minute now. She didn't misread the message from Malisa's hand either.

As if on cue, my father tugs on the hem of his double-breasted coat with gray pin-stripes, taps the blond swoop of his toupee as if he's asserting his dominance. Yet, I know who wears the pants in their family, *my* family.

Ugh!

I'm confident that the Powers only recognize those with wealth, which is why I don't even think twice about Malisa's indirect disrespect for my... Should I even call them my parents? Dr. Owens and Lydia seem like better alternatives. Malisa knows how to throw punches right back without even getting out of her seat, and I haven't even met her parents yet.

My parents bless Dr. Ellis with their front sights. Dragon lady crosses her thin arms then opens her beak and squawks, "Dr. Ellis, it's good to see you again. What exactly do we need to know about Blake?"

She's spoken to everyone but me.

"Well, hello to you too, Mother," I mock.

She swats away my statement as if there's an annoying gnat flying around her head. "I'll speak with you in a minute, Son. Let's find out what you need first." Somehow, I don't think my needs are usually her main concerns, and I'm certainly not wealthy if she doesn't even bother to reciprocate my dry greeting.

I cock my head, as if she's a piece in a museum that I'm trying to interpret, with no care if she never concedes my existence. She doesn't give me the impression that she's vital to it, unlike Astrid. Her, I don't think I can live without, not for very long anyway.

Dr. Ellis' stance grows rigid. "He needs a quiet environment, plenty of rest, no work. He's been put through a terrible incident and doesn't need to be goaded into remembering anything about anything or anyone, Mrs. Powers."

Oh, he just called her out for sure.

I don't think he likes her very much either. Neither do I, and I want to know exactly why.

She sniffs with conceited dripping from the gesture, going to do exactly what she wants to, regardless. "What *does* he remember?"

"Nothing about people or events, but he can grasp the right words to express himself appropriately. That's more than I hoped for with this type of condition, but the brain does its own thing. What's even better is he's using his common sense to work through the memory loss. His short-term memory is fine. Most things, he'll do because of muscle memory and knee-jerk reactions. Scents and people will trigger visions. He's already started getting images of his loved ones, but if you rush him into recalling anything, he'll get confused and start to believe your insight into things as gospel, when it's his perception that will stimulate his mind to reset itself."

Malisa snarls softly, and it's damn hilarious, but I reject the impulse to laugh.

"Why did I remember my parents first?" I blurt out. "If I couldn't remember my own name without it having to be told to me first by Mr. Lindsey, why would I vision the people who gave it to me first? They don't seem like people I'd eagerly associate with, even when related to them, not when they wear their narrow-mindedness on their sleeves."

My... Nuh huh. *The* parents—something about putting the 'my' in front of their status just isn't working for me—gift me the same look that I was harboring for the bulletproof vest. Astrid flinches in my side eye.

I've hurt her.

Unacceptable. My arms stretch out to her. Reassuring her is all I want to do, *must* do. Knee-jerk reactions, on point.

"You came soon after, Astrid. I promise, baby. The way you make me feel stuck with my hippo... whatever, even when nothing else did."

She circles the bed and embeds her palm in mine, her grip strong for such a small woman. The moisture in her eyes spills over her lashes, but the tips of her full lips boost upwards. A buzzing develops under my skin. It's like a million insects' wings are taking flight. The emptiness behind my rib cage fills up. Finally, what has been absent since I left the hotel is finally in its place—a connection with the woman I love on a molecular level that makes everything alright no matter how screwed up things are.

And plenty is unquestionably screwed up if Ashley and Martin Powers are my damn parents. Maybe even me.

It doesn't feel like I am at this moment though, and that's what counts, well, for me it does.

Scrutinizing everyone from behind his glasses, Dr. Ellis stashes the clipboard under his arm. "It's the hippocampus, Mr. Powers. The older memories usually come back first. Most patients going through what you are would've given their teeth to remember those who loved them this soon, and I don't think Astrid has been in your life long enough to be considered an old memory or flame. Do you feel like there's something's out of sync with yours and your parents' relationship, Blake?"

"Yes," my instincts field his question before I can even think about it. Malisa's, Astrid's, and perhaps everyone who's outside the curtain duplicate responses ride on top of mine, emulating a choir that is fully in tune for at least that one, single note.

The parents' resounding, mutual 'NO!' drowns us out, but who's going to believe them when the bulk of my visitors have already spoken?

Dr. Ellis blanches. "Uh, can I ask everyone to not respond unless spoken directly to? That's one of several reasons for the 2-visitor only rule... that's being *broken*."

"Thank God for Councilman Alder," Astrid sneers quietly.

The mother turns completely white. "Who?"

Astrid's eyes dart to me. "No one." Should I know Councilman Alder?

The mother points at Astrid with a trembling finger capped by a white-tipped talon, um, nail. "You said Councilman Alder. Is he the one that pulled the strings for you to visit *my* son when you're clearly not family?"

"Put your finger down, Mother," I demand quietly.

"Blake, that's your mother!" The father rebukes.

I cock one eyebrow.

Half-moons form on Astrid's high cheekbones when her eyelids condense, nose puckering at the bridge. "You'll have to ask Councilman Alder, Mrs. Powers"

The mother finally drops her finger. "No, I'm asking *you* did you talk to him, and you will answer me."

Astrid snorts.

"This is what I'm talking about," Dr. Ellis rumbles. "Blake can't handle the bickering. You are going have to find your happy places, people, until you can take this elsewhere."

The dropping of a pin can be heard for about two seconds before the mother's mouth expands, "But he shouldn't be alone with a head injury, right?" Her nails fabricate indentations in her arms, like she's truly worried, but her question is as rhetorical as they can get. She simply needs confirmation of what she's already knows, or thinks she does.

And she's totally up to something.

But what?

"I don't think he needs to be alone until he's had time to just familiarize himself with the here and now. What came before will come back later. I'm almost definite of it, Mrs. Powers."

One side of the mother's mouth crooks upward.

"How long will he need to familiarize himself?" The father pipes up. "Blake has responsibilities, Dr. Ellis." And what could those be?

"It could be a few hours to a few days to a few weeks or even months. Depends on his brain and his *stable* environment."

Astrid's slender fingers clutch mine tighter. "Is that all you're worried about, Mr. and Mrs. Powers? Getting Blake to take over your businesses for you and keeping your bloodline pure? He's never *worked* for you, and that shouldn't be your main priority in the first place. Your son. Doesn't. Know. Who. You. Are. Do. You. Even. Care?" Each word is stressed a little more as her anger mounts.

Dr. Ellis' head tracks the argument, listening and waiting for someone to say something revealing that they normally wouldn't when levelheaded.

I'm also guilty of letting Astrid shake my mother's tree, hoping something juicy will fall out of it. Plus, it's fascinating to watch her get pissy on my behalf, and interrogate my mother. Somehow, I'm emphatically certain that Astrid's more inclined to get pissy *at* me, and damn good at digging until she hits the bottom of any situation when she sets her mind to it.

The mother bats her false eyelashes that could be mistaken for wings. "Who are you to talk to me like that?"

"I'm the woman that's carrying the next heir to your fortune," Astrid jabs, with every intention to maim the mother where it would be felt the most, in her bank account. "You didn't see that coming, now did you, *Grandma?*"

I couldn't be prouder of Astrid for hitting her where it hurts. I got a nagging feeling that the mother has done that to me more than a time or two. Her just desserts have been served, but I better not have a damn brother.

Chapter Eleven

Blake

The mother gasps. "She called me grandma to her child, Martin!"

His face turns to stone then pats my mother's shoulder delicately, obviously doing it for appearance's sake. Then I'm racing down a road after a blue truck with lights flashing in my face. I don't know what that has to do with anything, but it must be important if my mind is evoking that scene at this moment.

"A blue truck. Who has one?"

Astrid exhales and closes her eyes. "I do. You used to work on it for me on Sundays. The last time you saw it, you were chasing me. You were always on my back about using one of the cruisers for work, but I wouldn't because I like driving my truck." So, she's a sheriff or a deputy too. The inside of a janitor closet flashes behind my eyes.

What the hell does that mean?

"Stop, Astrid. That's too much detail." Dr. Ellis' warning precedes Astrid opening her eyes slowly. I start to sink in them.

Malisa sniggers, "Not for this crisis, it isn't too much."

Astrid's truck means a lot more than just liking driving it if she chooses to put unnecessary miles on it. I'll even venture to say someone special gave it to her. People tend to treasure things when they're connected to another heart, but whose? I don't want to know. If she says it's a gift from one of her lovers, and you can bet your ass that they're all *past* lovers now, I'll go ballistic.

"Chasing you? Why in God's name would I do that?" I can come up with a reason or a hundred though.

She swallows, morose suddenly. "I was going back home after I told Malisa to tell you I was pregnant. It happened just today."

Hallelujah! Astrid is pregnant with my *son.*

That only leaves a few thousand questions, like why was she going back home.

Unless, she's not mine anymore.

Rage slaps me in the chest then drags its hooks downward. I quietly gag on the discomfort and struggle to ask, "We're not together?"

Astrid forms a singular, tight fist of our unified hands. "We are now, and that's all that matters."

We're together! Thank God!

I flop back on the pillows, with the picture of floating lavender and white balloons. Now, I know the colors that were chosen for Malisa's and Apollo's special day, and the only thing that benefits is the empty compartments in my head that are filling up with one fragment of data at a time. I never been happier to be hallucinating about latex that's getting away.

"You were *not* with my son yesterday!" Ashley howls, completely freaking the hell out. "That is not *his* child!"

"How do you know that... Mother?" I stumble over the last word.

"She's got eyes on you, Blake," Astrid says straight-faced. "That's how. And she knows we got back together today before Malisa and Apollo's wedding. Did you get a snapshot of the kiss I gave him at the reception, Ashley? You're probably pissed off that we've been together all day, too, huh? But you not as angry as you're going to be."

Mother sucks up oxygen, like a bull preparing to rampage.

Astrid's lip spike into a humorless crescent shape. "You should've hired your private investigator a year ago, Mrs. Powers, when the people that mattered the most to Blake were the only ones that didn't know about us. When I was making love to your son every chance I got in every corner of Arrow with this brown body that carries Blake's one-third black, white, and Haitian child. I've had my brown hands all over his pale skin that you think makes you better than me. Let me tell you what *your* son's skin feels like, silk, and it turns a blush color whenever he's inside me. It kills you that he left something behind in me that you coveted for the next princess in the Powers' line, but anytime you want to meet me on the other end of a DNA test, all you and your princess have to do is dial my number. It's too bad that all your money, superior attitude, and riding on your high horse won't change the fact that your son sullied your heritage with a mixed baby? You may deny my child and even disown yours if he decides to stay with me, but you'll never forget mine. When you're up on your high horse, my child's existence will ride with you. When you're posturing for society, he'll be in the back of your mind. When you're on your sick bed, getting ready to bust hell wide open, your last thought will be. Of. *My. Son.* But he will never know you."

"Astrid," Dr. Ellis cautions.

I want to clap.

My mother throws her hands up. "Shut up, girl! My son doesn't date the likes of you!"

"He did eight months ago!" a man yells in the hallway.

A chorus of 'Shut up, Tommy' rings out.

"That's *your* brother, Frank," a new voice cranks out condescendingly.

"He's *your* brother too, Luke Owens," Dr. Owens laments.

I file 'Cranky man is Luke Owens' for further reference, and train my sights on the mother. "I'm going to ask you only one time to keep the names to yourself… mother, or you will leave. You've been cut out of my son's life. Don't get cut out of mine's too."

Astrid steps closer to the bed. "No, Blake, let her throw stones. It's all she's got left after being a small-minded, old woman with prehistoric views and no access to the only person in this room that may be able to stand her. You lost your shot to be truly loved by someone, lady, because Little Blake is the only one in here who wouldn't know any better. I'm certainly not going to stand by and let you trick your son into thinking your relationship with him is that of beloved mother and son. He avoids you and his father like the plague, has his own apartment—"

"Astrid!" Dr. Ellis whisper-screams from his throat.

Instantly contrite, she looks at him. "I'm sorry, Dr. Ellis, but I'd rather Blake's memory never come back than he believes either of his parents have his best interests at heart. They don't!"

An eerie leer ghosts my mother's lips. "I assure you we do, Dr. Ellis. He can't be alone at least for a while, right? He could've forgotten how to cook and burn the house down with him in it. Then who would be blamed for that? I know you don't want to be liable for that. So… shouldn't he come home with us? Tonight, since I'm sure you need the bed for someone who's actually sick."

"His memory is missing, not his ability to function as an adult, and no one here will let him cook, bath, or sleep alone if Dr. Ellis thinks we shouldn't!" The level of Astrid's cadence rises, and I grow apprehensive about the welfare of her and my son.

My mother grins with all her teeth on display. "You don't know what all he's forgotten, now do you? And he's *my* son. Who can take better care of him than his parents?"

"Lady, I heard you don't know nothing about taking care of—"

I kiss Astrid's knuckles, more because I want to than to get her attention. The circus comes to town under my blanket again, and I have to use my forearm to block the physical reaction from touching Astrid, even in the most innocent of ways. "Calm down, sweetheart. She's my… mother. What exactly is she going to do to me? And you should be laid up, with your feet up, complaining about your cravings."

Fear ripples through her eyes. She shudders and leans toward me, bracing her weight on my thigh with her empty hand. I cover her hand with my other one.

Astrid blinks. "Blake—"

"I'm going to do what I've always done, Son… take care of you." mother butts in.

"She has never done that, Blake," Astrid snarls. "All she'll do is confuse you."

My mother clutches the pearls around her neck and leans back, her eyes standing wide and heavily-caked with mascara. "Confuse him about what? Where he belongs? What he should be doing with his life? Who *really* has his best interests at heart? Who'll give him everything that he needs just when he needs it? That can't be you, Astrid, when he didn't even bother to tell anyone in his *real* family about you or that baby, now did he?" Ashley's… I mean the mother's eyes rove over Astrid, contempt sitting plainly in them. "And you wonder why he forgot you."

Astrid bristles and straightens up, her hand slipping from my leg to become a miniature fist at her side, the open and honest care for my wellbeing in her face more enthralling than the sensations she incite in me without even trying. "He doesn't know you either, lady, and it's none of your business why you never knew anything about me and our son. I didn't realize until now how much of a favor Blake did us by *not* telling you about us, but he knew you would be the nasty bit—"

"Astrid," I call before she can finish. She's seems to be about to pitch herself over my bed headfirst, to get to the mother who's worn out her welcome. "It's alright, love. You shouldn't get this upset while pregnant. Or ever. Let me tell everyone what's about to happen. Tonight, Astrid is staying here with me. In the morning, everyone outside in the hall come back so I can meet you if you can. If you can't, I'll find you.

Tomorrow afternoon, I'm going home with… my… parents." Suddenly, I want to brush my teeth.

If the Powers were going to spill their motives for being here, they would've by now. I won't find out what they are up to while laying up in this bed, watching her and Astrid go back and forth either, with my instincts clamoring for me to get to the bottom of every underlying issue with them. It's a necessity that I go with them alone into their domain, to find out what they want from me before I rivet my life to Astrid's permanently.

"What?" Untainted terror outpours from Astrid's eyes. "No, Blake! Don't do this, please!"

Yeah, I'll be using most of my time tonight to persuade Astrid that it's for the best if I go with the Powers on a solo mission. Then I get a serious case of déjà vu. Solo missions are what got me here.

The mother scoffs loudly. Oddly, thinking of her as anything with mother on the end doesn't come off as habitual for me. So… who do I think of as my mother because it doesn't compute to my vacant brain that I didn't have one while growing up? And why isn't it Ashley who I think was there for me?

Well, you won't find out tonight, and your family needs you, Blake, so put that shit on the back burner.

"Shhh, baby. It's going to be fine, Astrid. Trust me."

"Fuck!" expels from her before her chin freefalls and teardrops hit the sheets.

I release her hands to sit up, scissor my legs on each side of her, and pinion her head against my shoulder while brushing away the tracks of her tears from her cheeks. "Everyone out!"

"Gutter and crude that one is," mother says snidely, while pointing at Astrid. "Should've known that's why Blake didn't tell us about you and *your* baby. Someone should get you a better hair dresser."

"I'd rather have the background that I got if yours made you the monster you are. And, someone like your *husband* should get you a sandwich stat and make you eat it instead of letting you henpeck him." Astrid's muffled reply bats my collarbone.

Heat blooms under the first layer of skin, igniting tiny campfires along my arms and chest, along with flare-ups of my anger. "Leave her alone, *Ashley*, or I'm going home with Astrid, period." I hold her tight against me with one arm, while modifying the blanket to cover my naked rear.

"You heard the man." Dr. Ellis cosigns. "Come back tomorrow at your assigned times. Blake, I'll see you in the morning. Please let the nurse give you an IV."

"No."

He hums under his breath, irritated. "Fine! Everyone else has to leave right now, or I'll call security. Sasha will take Blake's parents one way. Everyone else go the other. Come with me, Mrs. and Mr. Powers."

"Who gets put out of a hospital?" Tommy sighs noisily. "Can't take these two families nowhere."

"Goodnight, son," the parents echo saccharinely sweet, their sentiment and endearment ringing false. Finally, their heavy presences diminish from behind me.

"Goodnight, Son," drifts in from the hallway from Malisa's parents. My chest swells with thick emotions. I'm not ever going to get that type of affection from the Powers. Only a real parent that had a hand in a child's upbringing would risk calling someone else's child theirs, which means I've found my *real* parents, or rather they found me.

"Night, Dr. Owens and Lydia." But using their government names is too... formal. I decide I'll call them Mama O and Pops... if I ever meet them.

Someone sniffles.

"Ah, sweetheart, don't cry," Dr. Owens coos. "I told you everything is going to be fine. Just give him a little more time."

"Night, nephew," Tommy says.

I recall his voice from earlier. "Night, Unk," I say impulsively, as if I'm conditioned to call him that, while planting soft kisses along Astrid's crown.

"Ha! He knows me by nickname and not any of yours. I'm special." A bear and a badge flips into my head.

So, I've given everyone nicknames. Only I haven't thought of but three. Well, I'll just pass out more as I'm introduced to them tomorrow.

"Shut up, Tommy," Dr. Owens spouts instantly, a trained reply too, I think.

"You're definitely not the kind of special you're thinking of, Tommy, that's for sure," a woman with robustness in her speech replies. Whoever she is isn't a woman to be messed with, but then again, her response seems like one of Malisa's insults; harmless.

"That was rude, *Aunt Chrys*," Tommy says, his voice growing distant as feet ricochet off the hallway's tiles. She laughs.

"Apollo," Malisa wails. "I've sat down and I can't get up, and Blake is too doped up to help me."

He laughs his ass off while stepping through the curtain. "I'm here, love. Let's go." The chair's feet scrape the floor as she empties it, with Apollo's assistance. "Night, best man and bridesmaid," he hints, still dressed in his tuxedo. I catch his meaning immediately; we were a part of their wedding.

I grin. "Night, future best man." He chuckles.

Astrid begins placing random kisses on my face. "Wait for me, guys." Then she lifts her face to mine. "Blake, I have to go back with them to get my truck, clothes, and purse."

Malisa stops in the slit of the sheet. "Stay, Astrid. We got you."

"No, Malisa, everyone has done enough for—"

"We got you, sis. It's the least we can do after you pulled strings to get us all back here, so you don't get to worry about anything. Maybe, we couldn't get Blake home like we wanted to, but him being here with you and that mean ass nurse to watch over him is even better. He's safe from his conniving parents for a little while longer, and that's because of you."

"I made that call because it was the right thing to do, Malisa, not to gain perks with the Owens."

"I know that, Astrid, and that's why we all love you already. You kept our family together." This is the kind of family that I can get used to, again.

I gather Astrid into my body again and close my arms around her. "Give in, baby. I can see Malisa's stubborn streak all the way over here, and it's a mile wide."

Astrid giggles, and looks up at me. "Fine. Night guys, and I love you all too." Malisa blows a kiss then vanishes in the hallway. Astrid doesn't even see it.

It's hard to believe that we're alone. "Have you said that to me before?"

"No, I haven't." She swallows, her disposition morphing into that of regret. "But I should've though." Her guilt is almost tangible, but there's no room for it between us.

My neck bends to bridge our noses together. "You can make it up to me in any corner of Arrow of your choosing, and I love you too, Astrid."

Her mouth flaps open and close. Little puffs of air leak out. "You don't know that, Blake, and we didn't actually make love in every corner of Arrow. I just said that to piss your mother off."

"Now, that is funny, and I do know I love you. I feel it. Felt at the hotel after I woke up. Mr. Lindsey asked me my name, and the Powers—"

"Were the people who came to mind because they gave you your name, and your first memories will certainly contain them."

"Exactly."

"I get it. You don't have to explain the order of your memories returning, Blake, just hold me."

"Oh, I don't plan to stop, but listen to me. I don't have to remember every moment we spent together to know you're the woman for me. But, how do I know where to go from here if I don't know where I've been? Please trust me to come back to you by tomorrow evening from my parents' home. I'd take you with me, but I don't want you arguing with that woman constantly. It's not good for the baby or you. I hoped she'd say something revealing while you two went at each other's throats, but she's keeping her cards close to her chest."

"You know we used to do nosy cop, observant cop when we went out on calls together. You'd let me ask the questions while you read the accuser's body language. You could always tell who's lying much faster than I could. Shit, I'm not supposed to be telling you any of this."

"Too late, and I trust you to give me an unbiased view about everything you know. We would've had to do that when dealing with domestic disputes for sure, and I assure you that I know Ashley and Martin are up to something. That's what's bothering the hell out of you, but you can let it go. I want to know what is up their sleeves before I tell them 'no, but thank you' to their faces when they try to manipulate me at their home tomorrow. They deserve an answer from me face to face after giving me life."

She snickers. "They deserve a face to face answer alright, so they can feel the upmost pain when you walk away."

Astrid's eyes whip away just before Dr. Ellis walks in.

"Sorry, guys, I just wanted to talk to Blake without interruption for a minute. What I'm about to say probably breaks every oath I took to not get involved in any matter that doesn't concern my patients' immediate health. With that said, I think Mrs. and Mr. Powers are certainly going to be a problem in the *immediate* future for you both probably, and aren't to be trusted."

He crosses his arms, making the tails of his white coat spread out like wings. "I think you sense that too, Blake, despite what you've forgotten. Amnesiacs don't normally start remembering so much at one time, but like I said, the brain does its own thing. There is one thing we can depend on in these cases though, and that's the mind giving out information as needed, and it's like yours thinks something precious will be at stake if you don't remember fast enough. You struck me as a man who wants everything in order before you move on to the next phase in your life, which is probably why everything that is upside down in your world is coming back first. Be on your toes with your parents is my advice. I'll say goodnight for real now. If you need anything, there's a nurse's button velcroed to the left side of the bed. Sasha will get you settled in a private room for tonight as soon as one comes available, Blake."

"Thank you, Dr. Ellis." He nods then departs as quietly as he came, knowing much more than he's letting on.

The lights dim on the entire floor, leaving the miniature crystal lamp fixture over the bed forming a halo around Astrid's head. I'm unable to look away from the angelic depiction being created by such a little hell raiser. "This has been a long day, sweetheart... at least I think so anyway."

Astrid's lips bow inward, suppressing a grin.

"Lay down with me until Sasha shows up," I request, while my fingers frame her jaw and ears.

Her face splits wide open. "I thought you'd never ask."

Even pregnant, it's nothing to hoist her up. She sustains her balance by latching on to my forearms. Her knees bend, fork off in midair, and then dock on the mattress. I lie us down sideways then adjust my upper body into a slant across the mattress, giving baby Blake space to lay with us too. Happily, I'm trapped in the apex of her thighs that are supporting my waist and manufacturing a cozy niche for my arousal. Her heat is devastating, and I'm still not close enough to it. My pelvis bucks into her without my consent or hers, but dry-humping her isn't adequate either. Inside her is the only solution for what ails me.

Astrid lurches back and whimpers softly, closing her eyes tight enough for her eyelashes to scrape her cheeks. "You're asking for trouble, Blake." Undoubtedly something I do around her often. "And you're injured, love."

"Sorry about that, especially with the hospital staff milling around and can walk in on us any minute."

I'm really not apologetic though, but I quit moving and pray for strength to not do it again, shutting my eyes. Looking at her is only going to have the opposite effect on my stubborn system that's craving to take her right here. I don't really give a shit if anyone gets an eyeful of us making love, but Astrid might.

"Don't be sorry. I love your sex drive too. It matches mine."

A rattling in my lungs shatters the quiet, as I inhale, trying to gain control. "Talk to me."

"I can't right now," she groans, as if she's suffering with pigheaded lady parts too. It's only fair since my erection is only getting stiffer, incessant that I bury it within Astrid and *show* her how much we love her back. Telling her how much has already been taken care of.

Get some space from her, Blake, even if it's just mental.

"You can, Astrid. Tell me things about you that I don't know... uh, never knew."

"Okay. Give me a second."

The tips of my fingers convulse, not liking the restraint I'm using to keep them from ripping her underwear off then powering through her southbound lips. I begin to trace the formation of the northbound ones just to give my hands something to do. She has no clue how close my passion is to pulling me under.

"My mother and father met in the sixth grade. April's an elementary school teacher with biracial parents. Wesley's a mechanic, Haitian immigrant, with his own small business in Harr... Right before my mother went off to college, he proposed. She accepted. They would have a four-year long distance relationship until she came back home, two months pregnant with me. As often as they could get away from their

196

obligations, the distance was just the length of their arms from one another. They wanted more kids after my little brother, Ian, who's a year younger and a computer analyst in Georgia, but my mother's endometriosis and full hysterectomy took the dream of more children away from my parents. I've wanted to be a cop since my best friend's father came to Career Day in the fourth grade. He seemed really nice to a nine-year old, while explaining why law enforcement needs more good officers. I've always liked helping people, but I would learn the hard way that he wasn't talking to the girls in my class that day. He's one of the bigots in our profession and a police captain for the city of… my small town, so I had to set my sights on the county's Sheriff's Department."

"Was it that bad working in your hometown?" I know the answer, but I continue with the idle chitchat, or I'm going to fuck her and me both senseless. How she feels about her history with her job in her hometown is floating in her face, and she isn't fond of reminiscing about it, but dropping the lines of communication could be disastrous for me who's barely in control of my libido.

"That station is a breeding ground for little bigots in training, with no room for moving up for me and one other Caucasian female deputy, so I started searching for other jobs on the internet. Took me five years to find Arrow on a website for officers seeking employment outside of… my state with equal pay. Councilman Alder contacted me personally soon afterwards, asked me why I wanted to leave my job and where did I see myself in five years. Thankfully, my truth was what he was looking for out of thousands of applicants; experienced, clean, not looking for any handouts or hands up, and willing to start at the bottom of the pecking order again. He asked if I could transfer immediately, I screamed 'hell yeah, I could be in Arrow that night' in his ear. He laughed his ass off while telling me that I should take time to settle my affairs and be in Arrow in two weeks. It was too damn long for me. I despised my superiors and most of my co-workers, all diehard chauvinist pigs of course."

She tips her head back, and smiles. "And then, I was standing in your Sheriff's Department. I thought you were going to be the same as my friend's father at first, after the way you reacted to my showing up for work, but you turned out to be so much more than I expected. I was in love with you by the end of my first month here."

A mental picture pops up of me slamming an office door then snatching up a desk phone with several little plastic slots marked with names beginning with Council Member written before each one. Alder is probably the first one I called.

Apparently, I didn't want Astrid working for me either, and no one has to insinuate or hope I recall the reason why—I knew my heart was in trouble the minute I laid eyes on her, and it happened all over again when she walked into my room.

"Do you know I've fallen for you twice, Astrid?"

Her chin wobbles. A glistening develops around her pupils.

"Alright, guys," Sasha says before entering. "Only one patient is getting to ride this bed while I'm driving. Little lady, you'll be walking for insurance reasons. You're not covered by it."

Sasha arrives too soon, but having a door with a lock and four walls are worth her invasion.

Chapter Twelve

Blake

"Sweetheart, let me help you down."

Sasha waits stoically for Astrid and me to work together, getting her feet on the floor. When it's just my fingers intertwined with Astrid's, Sasha disappears behind my head and maneuvers the bed toward the hallway. Astrid keeps up with Sasha's ridiculous pace with no problem. I'd ask Astrid to finish her story, but I'm sure it gets X-rated from her stopping point, and may be too much for Sasha's ears.

We turn a corner, my eyes never leaving Astrid's. Sasha stops and sidesteps to open a door. Astrid's fingers unlace with mine so Sasha can control the direction of the bed until it's in its last resting place in a room much like the makeshift one I just left; simple with an armchair, a muted television mounted high on the opposite wall, rolling table, and a partially cracked door to the bathroom.

"Sheriff Powers, a nurse will be back in a couple hours to check your vitals. The bathroom is connected to another patient's room. Lock both doors before you use it. I'm sure you'd prefer a suite, but they're all booked up and no one requested that we switch you out with another patient, so you're stuck in this one."

"That's fine," I comment blandly, not looking for special treatment, just more privacy than what I had.

She smirks. "Please be fully dressed when the nurse makes her rounds at ten, and that goes for the both of you. Get some rest, Mr. Powers. Those pain meds are going to wear off soon and you don't want it to be in the middle of… us changing shifts when they do." Sasha walks out without a backwards glance, closing the door softly behind her after turning the sconces on the wall off. Tendrils of light slink around the bottom of the bathroom's door.

Astrid and I look at each other. "She is no fool," she says dryly, her humor evident in her eyes, along with the glare from the television.

"Right, now come lay beside me again before she comes back." I pat the empty side of the bed.

Astrid reaches for my hand then climbs up beside me, lying on her back. Instantly, my hand nests on her stomach that seems to be roiling towards me, while I post up on my forearm. Astrid isn't taking up even half of the mattress, but I still scoot over.

"And you wonder why we're always in making love in semi-public places, Blake. Your hands are always on me. Yeah, no, I shouldn't have told you that either."

"Yeah, no you shouldn't have," I mimic. "Now, I know it's okay to touch you when I want to, and there's a good chance you won't mind."

"I never mind, Blake." Then her waist swells out between us from an overly active baby.

"What the hell is he doing?" I ask, amazed by the rippling movements under her flesh that cements the baby's presence, even when he's not quite in this world yet.

Astrid's chin drops. "Getting close to his father. He's been doing it since we met up today. Keeping track of you, I would say."

In awe of my son's intelligence even in the womb, it's impossible not to tip over and kiss Astrid softly, thanking her for her part in his growth and keeping him protected, literally, with her body. I can't imagine how uncomfortable that gets at time.

"Thank you," I say against her lips.

Phantom fingers skim my nape, walking through my hair, making me shiver.

"No, thank you, Blake. If it wasn't for you, I wouldn't have him."

"If it wasn't for *us*, Astrid. We couldn't have done this by ourselves, but he won't make it to air without you. I don't need my memories to know who does the most sacrificing to give a child life. And I don't need to be a rocket scientist to know that we split at some point, but you had to be willing to see me again for this family to be together right now. I'm sorry for whatever it is that I did to—"

One finger lays across my lips, silencing me, then falls away. "Who said you get all the blame, Blake?"

"I had to have done something to make you leave me."

"It's not what you did, and technically, I didn't leave you. We weren't together in the boyfriend girlfriend sense when I went home. I just moved away. Whatever we had back then, and I still don't have a name for it, didn't work out because of what *we* didn't do. I didn't ask for more from you like I should've, and you didn't tell me things about you that I should've known. It doesn't have anything to do with me and everything to do with… Shit! That's too much info, I think. I don't know. I just want you to know that I hold no grudges about our time before. We didn't start out like we should've, so we couldn't go on like most couples would've after making a baby together. I admit that there were some issues between us. However, I got a feeling that you're about to fix what's broken on your end permanently, Blake. I just don't like how you're going to do it. It's not about me trusting you but the people who created you. You promised to do something about them *before* your accident. That was good enough for me. I couldn't ask for more after I didn't push for you to open up to me before I left, without leaving you at least a Dear John letter. I take the blame for how we ended up after I found out I was pregnant. Even with your injury, you're still trying to fix what *was* wrong between us. No, you fixed us. You're trying to fix what's wrong with your… Dammit, this is so hard. I just…" She looks away.

Distance and sadness bogarts their way between us. I can't stomach it, so I alternate her chin back to where it was.

"You just what, love?" I ask, when she's looking at me again.

"You can't trust your parents," her voice lowers several octaves as if we're plotting a crime. "Nothing they say will be the truth. Well, probably ninety-nine percent of it won't be, and I should admit that I don't know them from a hill of beans—"

"Neither do I," I quip then chuckle.

She slaps me across the chest gently and represses another smile. "Dammit, Blake! I'm serious. I know I'm not supposed to even give you hints about your former—"

"But you've been doing it the whole while, so I can guess that you're more afraid than you're letting show, and you shouldn't be."

"Maybe not but I am anyway. You're everything to me and baby Blake as you can see, and we don't want to lose you. I can share you with your parents, but they're not going to play fair."

"Thank you for telling me that, but I need you to let me cut the poison out of our lives, and…" I vacillate, bobbing my head from side to side. "I really want to know what are they're up to and why I think Dr. Owens and Lydia are better suited as parents to me, and why my mother reminds me of a reptile. I've been thinking of her as Dragon lady."

Astrid barks with laughter. "Your instincts are sharp even if your memory is spotty."

The full wattage of her mirth is brighter than any sun. Her happiness and baby Blake's are my sole reasons for living, and I'll knock down any obstacles that stand in the way of it. Talking about my parents isn't going to distract Astrid from her worries though. Focusing on what I'm doing to her body is what I want from her until tomorrow evening.

"I promise you, Astrid, that I'll come back to you as soon as my parents show their hands tomorrow. Who knows? Maybe they'll have a change of heart and decide that they want their grandson in their lives. Maybe they won't. We'll be fine either way."

"You already made me that promise today." Her eyes swoop down to my mouth. "You don't remember that though, do you?" The air gets dense and hard to inhale, and I'm walking the lip of a chasm. The lost parts of my mind have put me there.

Dammit, why am I only getting bits and pieces?

Hopefully, in time, I'll have them all and put together properly. Not being able to now is the equivalent of failing Astrid, and I've already made that mistake.

I shake my head, responding to her and clearing it of thoughts that won't benefit me. "But I know I meant it both times."

"I know," she says before her thumbs contort my chin downward.

Astrid

Blake has been giving me mild, infuriating kisses since the day he informed me that my uniform and perfume have been turning him inside out for months. That's also the day I made my first mistake with him; I took his body instead of asking where would our relationship go from there. Ending up in a rip tide of what I thought would be just a casual fling for him, impossible to escape unless I swam with the current in a diagonal direction, methodically working my way back to the safety of land. I had a pretty damn good excuse why swept his desk clear with one hand first, then plant my bare ass in the middle of it after he came clean with me about his feelings. I slowly lose my mind anytime I'm in his company. That's why I jumped headfirst into his ocean without checking the depths.

He's been afraid I'll shatter when making love ever since, no matter how many times I tell him that I'm not fragile. Rough is good for the greedy woman he turns me into whenever he makes me wait to have him, and yes, I've tried to devour him a time or two... hundred. Tonight will be no different, and I always start with his mouth, after rolling him onto his back. Engaging in warfare with his tongue satisfies some of the yearning for him that builds until it sits like boulders on my nerve-endings.

He groans, as usual when I give him hostile kisses. Tenderly nipping at his lips. Sipping from the tip of his tongue and drawing circles around it with mine, completing the first step into coercing him into using his body to fuck me mindless. There is nothing soft about him. Constantly flexing muscles mold his physique like expertly laid bricks, but he's steadfast about being gentle with me. As much as I love his protective nature, it only makes me half savage. I want him out of control, holding tightly onto me as his anchor.

I halt the kissing to crawl down the outside of his body, and drive his blood to the surface of his neck with the suction from my mouth. Tickling his ear with my shallow exhales. Drawing lazy figure eights around his nipples until his hands are fisting my hair and cursing low in his throat. I move south, with the bed creaking under my movements, and smile against the indentations and valleys of his torso. Nowhere near the beast mode I'm trying to coax out of him, Blake relaxes, with his bent elbow cuddling his head. *Stubborn man.* Every one of them has a breaking point. It's a little further down, lounging on the fifth and sixth stump of his eight-pack.

I tug his gown out of the way to get to his manhood. Angry veins pucker beneath the surface. Angling my head and relocating my knees between his legs, I slurp at the head of his shaft, ingesting a tiny bead of his salty pleasure. Blake's hips jet upwards, feeding me more of his length, belting the back of my throat, his nails suddenly scratching at my scalp. It's a pity he'll let me savor him a minute or two longer before he reminds himself that I haven't cum first. A gentleman in just about everything he does.

"Shit, Astrid, up and off." And there it is. "Bend over the chair against the wall."

With his wrists grazing the outside of my breasts, I back off the bed. Barefoot, I pad to the oversized wingback with scroll arms. He stalks to the door, activating the lock, while I assume the position. The second I shut my eyes, he's frisking the backs of my thighs, squatting naked behind me. Although startling the hell out of me, my core knows it's him, grinding on itself, more than ready for what comes next.

"God, Blake! You're too damn stealthy!"

He laughs low, arrogantly. "And you're going to have to be quieter like a cat too, love."

"Not possible with you."

Fingertips slip under the thin strings of my nude-colored panties then pause. "Why do I keep recalling a janitor's closet, Astrid?" Another flashback. Good. He'll be back to his old self in no time at this rate.

"There's one at the Sheriff's department, next to your office."

"Did we sleep together there?" Many, many times.

I peek over my shoulder. "You tell me, big boy." I'll sabotage the Powers all day long to prevent their puppeteering of their son, but I want him to recount our history on his own, or being with him will seem counterfeit to me. That'll break my heart.

He raises an eyebrow, purses his lips, and stands up, already aware of when I'm taunting him. Detests things being withheld from him. I do it often, just so he'll exact a cost that I'm only willing to pay my way.

"You're not going to tell me, are you?"

I face the wall. "Nope. What we have will be real to you, even if I have to torture you with evading your questions the whole time we're together, Blake."

"Suit yourself," he says too damn nonchalantly.

Oh shit!

The tearing of my panties assaults the quiet, the twenty-third pair he's destroyed. A moan rents the air for space. Yep, that would be me, and I'll only get louder.

Blake fondles the entrance to my body with his tip. "So fucking wet." Then he plows into me, up to the hilt, and stalls out, needing more space than my body has.

"Oh shit!" My locked knees wobble, stomach curdles, and lungs contract under his carnal attack, contradicting my love for the barbaric manner he's quite capable of when I can strip him of his gentleness. I never said I could handle him when he's like this though, just enslaved to the extreme satisfaction his undisciplined behavior dishes out.

"Astrid, you've got to be quiet, baby."

"Blake," I pant, "you're impaling my ribcage, asking for the impossible, and don't you dare stop again."

"What about the baby? I don't want to hurt him."

Lord have mercy.

"He's fine, sweetheart. That's what my womb is for. I may even need you to kick off my labor if I go past my due date on the 30th of next month, so don't chicken out on me. I promise having sex is more than okay while I'm pregnant. Consult my doctor if you don't believe me, but do it tomorrow. Right now, I need you. I'll even be quiet." Not. But what's a little white lie going to hurt? He'll check any fuss I make himself anyway.

When he doesn't continue making love to me, I glimpse at him who's imitating a Greek statue behind me, beautifully sculptured and immovable.

Alright then, I'll take matters into my own hips.

After closing my legs, forcing him to widen his, I reverse bounce off his washboard abs. Euphoric sensations begin to bombard me and apply pressure to the most sensitive areas, uncaring that I'm currently filled with lust. Too much stimulation and I'll climax. Not yet. He's still in control somehow.

My walls clamp down on his shaft like vice grips and drag along the base of it. He clutches at my expanded waist and slings his head back. His jaw develops a tick, muscles strain, color of his skin changing to the rosy hue that betrays his mindset; he's already in paradise. No beaches, waterfalls, horizons, or sea waves roiling on and off the sand are needed for us. It's almost perverted how much enjoyment I'm getting out of watching the crumbling of his bullheadness.

Doesn't matter where I'm at with him, Heaven tracks *me* down. I always forget to account for the boomerang effects of my own bedroom tricks. On the verge of succumbing to them before him, I have to gnaw on the inside of my cheek to hush myself. The lace of pain from my teeth only provokes the pent-up orgasm. It goes berserk, pummeling my soft tissue crammed with Blake, adamant about being unleashed. I clench every muscle I have and the frame of the chair, determined to outlast Blake.

"Baby, damn," spews from him just before he rocks into me, but he's still civilized.

Dammit, where is this man's heathen side?

He frees my breasts from the restraints of my bra, and latches onto them. Using them to lock me into a much too sweet-tempered tempo.

But he's moving, Astrid. He'll give in soon. You can hold on a little longer.

The pep talk is nothing more than a bunch of baloney. The slapping of our flesh while he hits my delicate spots, even at this pace, is mind numbing, wearing me down. Energy depleting way too fast. Soon, there won't be enough to wait for Blake to crack *and* maintain imprisoning the monstrous climax desperate to be set loose.

I'm practically dying to cum, contemplating surrendering to my needs, and drooping forward. Something's got to give, and it's going to be me. Kneecaps go first, burdening the outer rail of the chair with my weight. Next, my elbows bow down, dropping like concrete blocks. I tremble as if I'm on a caffeine high. Blake's motion ceases. He pats my shin.

"Get up on the chair, baby."

I deposit a knee against the arms of chair's sides unhurriedly, thankful for the extra space in it, scared if I move too fast, I'll lose the bit of control I have over the suspended orgasm.

He taps my lower back. "Now, arch for me."

I submit to his command, placing my hands on the cushion, permitting total access to my soaking wet tunnel I pray he exploits. He carves handles out of the globes of my ass, and then drills into me. Not expecting the harsh impact, it throws me over the cliff that I've been teetering on for far too damn long.

"Blake! I'm—"

He gags me quickly with his palm, while towing my ass backwards one-handed, right into the path of a powerful lunge of his pelvis. I roar behind the shield of his fingers, enduring the hammering of his body and the hell reigning down on mine. He's broken at last, at the wrong time, when I'm tolerating more bliss than a human should, and not going to survive it.

Self-preservation kicks in, instructing me to take the fetal position and repent my sins while I still have the chance. Basically, I'll be bending over to kiss my ass goodbye. Seems appropriate, so I stow my head in the crook of the chair. Blake plunges into the middle of the hurricane raging inside me, crashes through white-hot spots, then falls back, and repeats. The storm intensifies. This isn't going to turn out well for me.

It was stupid to bury your head and leave your ass uncovered in the first place, Astrid!

Now you tell me.

Abort fetal position now, dummy!

I rise, locking my elbows, lessening his penetration along with my chances for suffering back to back orgasms. Blake seizes my forearms, folding them behind my back. Jesus, he's subduing me. Too weak to resist, I decide groveling is in order.

"Blake, if you don't stop, I'll cum again. Too sensitive."

He puts pressure on my spine, which I cave under like wet paper. "Not yet, Astrid. Too good."

I wholeheartedly agree. "That's why I need you to stop, sweetheart. I can't handle another—"

"No." He rams into me, rudely cutting me off. "Way." His momentum picks up. "In." Spring boarding off my backside, he spears through me. "Hell." Inciting a rippling effect of cruel, punishing waves that I'm unfit to ride out. "Cumming too." He's not the only one. "Fuck, Astrid. It almost hurts." Karma is a bitch.

He burrows balls-deep in my sheath, grabs for the wingback, chugging oxygen. Thoroughly screwed and protected by my barbarian, I submerge my teeth in my bottom lip, smothering the acoustics exploding from my voice box. My arms ooze down beside me, as if they're made of goo. I don't know how long it takes for the climax to taper off, but I'm completely spent when it does and my right mind returns. Blake is standing beside me, all supreme, perfect, and functioning. Now how is that fair?

"Up, Astrid."

My thighs quiver, recommending that I stay right where I am or deal with the consequences. "No thank you very much, love. Just leave me. I'll get up when I'm not a wreck." Grime coats my throat like I've been eating ashes.

"Nope. Bath time."

"I'll drown, but you can throw the water on me, and I'll suck it out of my clothes. Doubt if I can hold a cup."

Blake laughs. "Nope to that too. Just lift your head, and I'll do the rest. Quickly, sweetheart, I need to unlock the door so Malisa can come in with your luggage."

"Forgot about her. When did she arrive? Why did I not hear you answer the door or her knocking?" I slap the arm posts and shove upright.

"She got here about thirty seconds ago, and you had your shoulders hunched up to your ears like you were practicing a tornado drill." Oh.

He scoops me up and enters the bathroom, small with the bare necessities. The straightaway between each entry point isolates the shower with a seat from the sink and toilet that Blake parks me on. Waking up my bladder. He fiddles with the knobs for the shower, regulates the temperature, and smacks my forehead with his lips before securing and shutting the doors. All normal activities for us that I won't take for granted, not after I could've lost him today. We're fortunate it's just his memory that's been snuffed out and not his life. Blessings counted.

Now, how in the hell am I going to explain to him that I go back to work tomorrow, cleared for duty to show him the ropes in his own station, in exchange for the favor Councilman Alder did me? Somehow, I don't think Blake is going to be on board with it while I'm carrying his child or anyone else's, fully-functioning hippocampus or not.

Chapter Thirteen

Blake

It's mesmerizing observing her sleep, and sort of creepy when you think about someone lying next to you, making sure your breathing doesn't stop while running a fingertip over every reachable inch and listening to your heartbeat. Oh, and laying their head and hand on your stomach from time to time just to see if the baby you carry will react.

So, I'm creepy, because I sure as hell couldn't stop myself from doing it, and I don't think my kid sleeps.

Astrid hasn't moved since I bathed her and rummaged around her luggage for something for her to sleep in. At least, somebody is sleeping around here. I can't get back to it, since I jerked awake at three a.m., after dreaming I was a driver treading shark-infested waters. Yeah, I'm contributing that nightmare to the Powers, too. Watching Astrid nap isn't the only thing I'm doing. Deliberating about what the parents will try today with my head operating on half a tank is the other. I'm tense and edgy. Gazing at Astrid and playing with the baby is my feel-better serum.

The trilling of her phone from her purse under the garment draped over the chair interrupts my stalker moments. She smiles in her sleep, opens her eyes, then flips over on her side. "Why aren't you sleeping, baby?"

"Because, I can't look at you if I'm looking at the back of my eyelids, baby."

"You've been watching me *sleep*?"

"Yep, and playing with the baby. And I like doing it. And I like waking up to you two."

Her shoulders bob and weave with her noiseless humor. "You know it's usually even… hmmm… you almost got me."

"Tell me," I insist just to hear her talk. She's already revealed when we usually wake up together, evening, and I can see us getting ready for work together. Yes, I actually see it.

"Uh uh. Remember, so I don't feel like I've planted memories of us and have you because you don't know any better."

Now, this is a good woman who wants what she has honestly. Then her standing in the station in civilian clothes on her first day at ASD comes back to me. I'm not any happier about it now than I was then. Don't want her facing down three burglars and maybe being bashed in the head. To lose her like that would make living not worth the effort. Still, I'll do what she thinks is best for her.

Astrid's face falls. Her hand strokes my shoulder. "Blake, what is it?"

"A memory… of you, and lady, you would have me even if I never remember. You keep stealing my heart at first sight."

She blinks rapidly, more moisture clustering in her eyes every time she does it. "Thank God."

"Exactly." I kiss her softly on the lips and back away, before scooting closer to her, wrapping my arm around her. "Now why is your phone's alarm going off? What exactly do you have to do at seven in the morning?"

Her mood swings to grave, honey-hue pupils less lively. "Get ready for work. I have to be there at nine."

I gulp down air. She won't be here to see me leave with the Powers, or wait for me to come back to her at wherever she goes to from here. It hurts.

And it's selfish to want her all to yourself, Blake.

What can I say? I'm spoiled after last night.

"Where are you working?"

"ASD."

I get out of the bed to stand beside it. "How long has this been set up?"

She sits up. "Since I asked Councilman Alder to intervene with the hospital so the Owens and I could see you yesterday. Your parents and the hospital's regulations would've left us standing at the front doors."

"I believe you, but you should've lead with this at least when we got in here last night, if not when you got to my first room." Behind my eyes, every moment of us battling to find common ground after I stupidly hid shit from her zoom in from every which way. "Keeping secrets is *not* good for us, Astrid."

"I know. Didn't want to ruin the night or set you off… like I've done."

"Doesn't make it okay. We've been through this before. I almost lost you because of shit like this."

"I didn't say it was okay, Blake." She inhales loudly. "How do you know…"

I rap my temple with my index finger. "You seem to be my brain's muse for wanting to work like it should, and going back to ASD without me is *not* alright with me."

"Blake, I'm still a trained deputy."

"I know that. I'm proud of it, but you working alone worries the shit out of me, Astrid, especially when you're pregnant." Here comes the part where I let her do what's best for her, and I hate it. "I need to put on some clothes. The parents sent some at about six. Sasha didn't like being their delivery woman either. Copper sent over my keys and phone and left my truck parked at my apartment, wherever that is."

Astrid follows my movements toward the chair. "Jesus, Blake, don't change the subject and leave this argument unfinished between us."

"It's not an argument, baby. We just agree to disagree about what you're going to do, and I am—

"Going to walk away before we find a compromise. How does that solve anything?"

I stop in my tracks halfway across the room. "How do we compromise, love? I can't stand even thinking about you being in danger out there by yourself. If someone even breathes on you…" It's best if I don't even go there right now.

"Blake, you listen to why Alder asked me to work at ASD again and—"

"And then I'll magically understand and be completely fine with it? No. Astrid, baby, I have half a mind and I'm only half the man I think I was right now *because* of ASD."

A flurry of the bed linen being pitched aside so Astrid can get to her feet much swifter than she should be able to do occurs. A very capable woman, with her chest puffing in and out rapidly like she's trying not to spontaneously combust, stabs the air between us with her finger. "Don't you fucking say that, Blake! Ever! You're the kind of man that every man should aspire to be, even with most of the blanks in your head, and I love you and my father because of it! Now are you going to listen to me or just be all overprotective and shit?"

She's too distraught for her and the baby's welfare, and just as adorable as a kitten would be trying to take on a full-grown bear.

She's still furious. You did it, so fix it, moron.

I'm trapping her front against mine before the thought has ran its course. She bearhugs me back, chin in my chest.

"I didn't say anything, Blake, because I didn't want you to be mad."

"Hmmph, well, I am. Can you understand why?" She nods. "Now, tell me why Councilman Alder thought he should hire you without consulting me first… *a-freaking-gain*," I huff.

Dammit, why can't my past come back all at one time?

It's frustrating to be in a critical moment when snippets of my life blast through me, like now.

She giggles. "Are you having flashbacks every second?"

"No, but it would be better if I was. Now, tell me about your deal with Councilman Alder."

"He didn't consult with you, Blake, because he can't. You won't even recognize him, and he doesn't think it'll be wise to just walk up to you and start talking shop. That's why he rehired me. Yes, I can still go on calls if I want to, but Arrow isn't a hotbed of crime. Deputy Miles should be able to keep the peace until you're ready to. In the meantime, I'm the go-between for you and the council members, and hopefully I'll get you back to a fully effective Sheriff. He doesn't want to replace you, so I get to do for you what you did for me when I moved here, train you until it all comes back to you." That, I can live with.

"Sounds like Councilman Alder has a good head on his shoulder. I'm so sorry for not hearing you out first. I should also confess that I had this idea that you'd stick by me until I was discharged, and then you could go to my apartment and—"

"Wait for you there," she says snidely. Yeah, no she's not going for that.

"Yes. I'm spoiled, Astrid. And you're my everything, and everything is fine when you're near, no matter what's happening, but I'm still going to let you live your life. I just need you to promise me something though. No going on calls alone. If Copper isn't available, you don't go.

Arrow may not be a hotbed of crime, but it's picking up. The three dead men I woke up beside says so."

"No calls alone. I can do that. We just compromised. How are you dealing with the shootings, Blake?"

"I'm not. It isn't bothering me, and that's probably because I don't remember killing two men. I think if I did, I'd feel some type of way about it."

"You would feel some way because you'd rather not hire any deputies, putting them in danger. Instead, you work two shifts alone. If you killed someone, it's because they presented a real threat to you that you couldn't fix without pulling the trigger. But the department has a psychiatrist that you'll be required to talk to before being cleared for duty again. For now, we just need you to remember the officer's conduct, codes, and how to operate as Arrow's Sheriff again. And there's no rush. Your term isn't up for two years and you have me, standing right beside you even when I'm not."

"We just made it through our first real argument, Astrid." Peace washes over me. Everything is still as if it's saving its breath in one of those instances when I should be kissing the hell out of her, so that's what I do, until someone knocks on the door. Roughly against her mouth, I say, "Come in."

Of course, she snickers against mine, laughing *at* me and not *with* me. I couldn't care less. Baby Blake kicks the shit out of both of us, and makes her cackle harder. I'll take that as he doesn't appreciate the disturbance either. The door opens, admitting a couple. Two different shades of brown complexions complement each other from the cautious faces of the people. Their devotion for one another billows off them like smoke surrounding me. This is how I'm supposed to feel around family, loving. Definitely Mama O and Pops.

A plastic sack with takeout trays swings from Mama O's hand. "Morning, Blake and Astrid."

Pop echoes her sentiment.

"Morning, Mama O and Pops." I release Astrid to embrace them both.

When I step back, Mama O dabs her eyes. "You remember us."

I don't. The last thing I want to do is disappoint them. "No, I don't, yet, but I recall your voices from last night. I'm sorry. I just thought it would be too proper to call you by your government names. I hope that's alright, since you're the ones that really raised me, right? I just got this feeling that you did."

Pops sniffles, and lugs his wife into his side. "Your feeling is correct, Son, and Mama O and Pops is what you've always called us. Nothing to be sorry about."

"Well, that's great, because things were about to get really weird for us all... like wearing this gown with my butt out while meeting you." The room fills with their amusement while I reach back, tugging the edges of the hospital gown closed. "Let me get dressed and we'll spend a little time together before breakfast comes."

Mama O extends the sack to me. "We brought breakfast. The first two trays are yours. We're not going to stay long. Everyone wants to drop by at some point in pairs so you'll at least get a glimpse of their faces."

All kinds of faces come forth through the fog hanging over me. Mama O and Pops is one of them, and I'm not always a grown man when I see them.

"Thank you." I take the bags from her hand, finally, and pass it on to Astrid, who foists them off on the bed.

"Go on, Blake. I'll bring your clothes to you," she offers, still in her frilly nightwear that covers her from neck to toe.

"Thanks. I really didn't want to flash anybody. The gown is barely covering me, and Mama O might mistake it for me misbehaving and smack me in the back of the head for it just for old time's sake. I have enough head injuries as it is."

Tears stream down the cheeks of the only real mother I've known. "Still a damn clown even with Alzheimer's at twenty-seven years old."

"That's Unk's fault," I point out.

Pops drapes his body over Mama O's, his eyes reddening, as he swallows her small frame. I don't have to tell him that my recollection of them is coming back. He seems to just know things. "I believe that, Son. You spent maybe too much time with Tommy. Now, go get dressed because we don't have much time before two more members of your family show up before your blood relatives do, and we'd rather not be here for that. We might actually be escorted out of here by security next time."

"I won't be here either, guys," Astrid adds. "Have to go to work, so we probably need to find someone to be here with Blake when the Powers show up. We need to combat their shadiness as much as we can before he's alone with them."

I love when this woman tries to shelter me. Hauling her into my side, I kiss the top of her head. "Don't worry about me, guys. Don't go out of your way to babysit me. I need to learn to deal with the parents."

Mama O wobbles her head. "You would say that. Never expecting extra from anyone for yourself, except food. You haven't changed at all."

"Is that good or bad?"

"It's good, Son," Pop says, with a huge grin.

Astrid starts petting my back. "Go get ready, baby. I need to get ready too. And there are quite a few Owens."

"Okay, don't leave yet, Mama O and Pops." I reverse toward the bathroom.

"Never," she says sadly.

After Astrid delivers my outfit, I encourage her to eat while I get my hygienic acts out of the way. I have no issues with performing them correctly. Something else to be grateful for. Unzipping the bag, I find a black suit and dress shirt with leather loafers, along with boxers and a tie. I'm not pleased, a tee-shirt and jeans kind of guy who needs briefs to prohibit his junk from swinging everywhere. Since it'll be an imposition on someone to go get my own clothes and I need to play the part the parents want me to, I put on the damn suit. Highly inconvenienced, I enter the room where Astrid has just finished up scrambled eggs, bacon, and toast, and draining a plastic tumbler of water.

Approaching the bed, I wonder whether she ever had morning sickness. Astrid's mouth drops open midchew. Mama O and Pops are seated in the single chair, as they normally are, her in his lap with their jaws on the ground too. I sit beside Astrid. "Did you ever have morning sickness?"

She swallows. "No, and I answered that because you wouldn't know that at all."

"You left right after you found out you were pregnant. I know." And I'd love to forget it.

"You look beautiful, Blake," she says bleakly.

My head drops to the side, as I palm her cheek. "You don't sound too happy about that."

"You just seem to fit right in with your parents, and I have to admit it's heartbreaking, but I know you'll come back to me."

"Damn straight, and this thing is uncomfortable. I'd have someone go get my clothes for me, but I think I should leave the suit in place for a front for the parents. Since you're going to be at work, I thought I tell them to come get me after the Owens are through visiting."

She dusts her hands free of crumbs over the plate. "I get it, babe. You want to get this over with. If you want to cut out on them early, just call me. I'm in your contacts."

"I know, love. I went through my phone last night, and guess what? I can still read."

Astrid playfully slaps at my chest. "Silly."

"Every day," Pops groans, and lifts Mama O to her feet. "We'll be going now. You guys need some time alone. Luke and Natalia have already called, wanting in here. Come by the house, you two, as soon as you have time. I'm usually at home by six. Lydia is there all day sometimes. We'll get out your hair now so someone else can get in it."

More hugging before they leave, Astrid communicating her goodbyes first before she gets ready for the day. My attention is pasted to the bathroom door, while I eat, as she does whatever women do in the morning before work.

Last night, after she dozed off as soon as her head hit the pillow, I imagined it would be her clinging to me before I left with the parents. Yeah, well, I think it's going to be me doing the clinging in about half an hour. Do I want to talk her out of going to ASD? Hell yes! Am I going to? No.

She comes out in a purple maternity dress at the same time someone raps on the room's entrance. A man with the similar build as Pops and much gruffer air about him answers my, "It's open."

He steps to the side, so an elf-sized Native American woman can walk in. She cuddles a toddler who's a cross between his parents on her hip. They all say, "Hey, Blake." Their faces emerge on the porch of a house that I took Astrid back to after chasing down her truck.

"Hey, Uncle Luke, Natalia, and Jr. Why haven't I started calling you Aunt Natalia yet?" That seems to break the ice for her who charges me, limbs too short to reach completely around me.

"Because I wasn't in the immediate family when you started calling everyone uncles and aunts. You were a teenager when I married Luke, and aunt just never got tacked on to my name. I don't mind though," she murmurs against my shoulder, with Uncle Luke hanging over hers. I'm not the only one who's overprotective.

"Well, I mind, Aunt Natalia." That's enough to make her cry and Uncle Luke hug us both.

Each meeting with the Owens will go the same way. Two adults, their children if they have them, will totter in carefully, as if they're walking on eggs. Then someone starts weeping. I'll have at least one to five flashbacks for each new face. It's not all my memory, but it's something. Then Astrid looks down at her cellphone from her place on the bed, and announces that it's time for her to leave. I plant my mouth on hers before she can say anything else. When Astrid flattens my willpower to let her go, she backs off.

"Shit, Blake." She fans herself. "I'm seriously thinking about calling in on my first day after that."

"I won't be mad with you if you do." I receive a smack across the chest for doling out my approval.

"I'm sure you wouldn't, but Councilman Alder is probably already on the way. It wouldn't be good to stand him up. I need to prepare for your first day too, and I have no idea when that is going to be or what I should be doing. I do know it's going to be torture being in your office when you're not there. That's going to be new for me, and I don't like it, but it's good I have somewhere else to be because I'll probably try to strangle your mother." There is that.

"What if I meet you at the station? I don't want to go home without you, and you can show me around my own apartment."

"Hmmph, I bet you'll want to find the bedroom first too, huh?"

"Of course. What red-blooded man wouldn't when they have a woman like you?"

"Typical."

"You probably say that about me a lot, don't you?"

"No. You're one of the few good ones, and that's why it is so easy to love you, but I have to go, baby."

"Okay." I move back, so she can approach the door. "You should let me walk you out now before I don't let you go period. There *is* a bed behind me."

She beats a path to the door. "And a chair," she says smugly before entering the hallway.

"Woman, stop it."

She smiles back at me, and I give it some serious thought to kiss her until she says to hell with ASD. I settle for placing my fingers on her spine until we reach her truck where the sun and soft breeze play in her curls.

"I love you, Blake."

"I love you more, sweetheart." I help her in, then watch the Denali's brake lights until they disappear. Yep, I don't like this at all. I should be with her. Instead, I must play the good son to the bad parents.

Inside the hospital, I stop at the nurses' station and ask them to ring up Dr. Ellis. Sitting here waiting alone, when all my family have come and gone, just doesn't appeal to me. I find it abnormal that none of my blood relatives have come by. I only demanded that the parents come back in the evening. What would I have done if I hadn't had the Owens and Astrid? It's a wonderful thing that I'll never know.

Sasha replaces the phone on its base. "Dr. Ellis is on his way to you in twenty minutes, Mr. Powers."

"Thank you." I extract my phone from my front pocket and scroll through the missed calls list until I locate the mother's number. From the double digits sitting by their individual numbers, it's rare for me to pick up when they're summoning.

Dragon Lady answers on the second ring. "Hello, Son. I do hope you feel better today." Her well-wishes are warm, but icicles form on my arteries anyway.

"Hello, and I do. Dr. Ellis is about to discharge me. You can come get me now. Might as well get this over with."

"Excellent, Blake. We have so much to talk about. Lacey, call the driver around."

"What exactly do we need to talk about?"

"Why don't we talk about it when we're face to face?" What difference does it make?

"Well, I'm good with discussing it now."

"I'm not, Blake. We should all be together like we used to be."

I expect the sparking of moments of the time when a family gathering occurred. Nothing. She's lying. How far will she go along with it? "When was that? Specifically, when I was an adult, if that makes it easier for you."

"All the time."

Inside my room, I plop down in the chair. "Like when?"

"Blake, this is *not* helping your condition. You're supposed to remember stuff like this on your own. I'll see you in twenty minutes. Goodbye."

"Seriously, how did her teeth not fall out her mouth after the explosion of lies from her tongue?" I ask my screensaver of a grinning Astrid in uniform, then hustle the phone back into my pocket before I change my mind about looking into the Powers from the inside. I blow air toward the ceiling.

What have I gotten myself into?

I should be proposing to Astrid instead.

Chapter Fourteen

Blake

Dr. Ellis is much quicker at discharging me than he is at diagnosing. Yeah, that's how it's supposed to be. However, I'd rather be going to Astrid's truck than the parents' limousine illegally parked in front of the lobby doors. I swear I'd write them a ticket, if I knew how to. For someone that wants me in their lives badly, neither parent got out the car to hear what I can't do until my injury is healed, which is just about everything.

An aging chauffeur exits the car and opens the back door. "Hope you feel better soon, Mr. Powers." Nelson Thurman. His name is all I know about him; besides the fact that he's been with the Powers since I was a child. That's all I ever knew.

"Thank you, Nelson." I climb inside to the stares of the parents beside me, smiling like they've been botoxed.

Are they even capable of real emotions?

Doubt it.

Nelson closes the door the second I notice the dark-haired man on the seat under the tinted divider. His white suit is tailored. The cost of it could feed a family for a year. He looks more like my father than I do. Well, how Martin would look if he was healthy, that is. I get an instant headache from a surge of pictures coming in fast and furious, my temper rising with each one.

"Camron," I say blandly. I've known him for most of my life too, and he's no better than the parents.

He grins. "Yep, it's me, cousin."

I don't return the gesture. "What are you doing here?"

"I heard about the incident and came to make sure my favorite cousin was good."

"Why?"

His smile slips. "Because we're family, Blake."

"Are we? We haven't talked or been in the same room since we were twelve, on the last annual trip I took with the parents to Italy for a meeting at the parent company. You've lived in New York for eight years since you left Italy, graduated Stanford University, and opened an extension of the Powers' empire in Candleton, New York. I'm relearning that this family doesn't show up unless there's something in it for them? So why are you really here?"

"Blake!" Dragon lady rumbles. I ignore her, didn't sign up for making nice with anyone, just find out what they're up to, and advise them to get lost afterwards.

Camron glances at the parents. "Because Ashley and Martin called me and asked me to be here. I'm truly concerned about you, Blake, and the Power's empire belongs to you too."

"No, it doesn't. I explicitly said I never wanted to work for the *empire*, and yet, the first thing the parents do is try to immerse me in it after I damn near get my block knocked off on the job."

"That's because you shouldn't be working that job anyway," the mother says patronizingly. "It's beneath you. It's time to step up to take your place at the head of your family. We've let you have your time as Sheriff. It's time you give up on that little job and come back where you belong."

"Let me? Being Sheriff is what I love to do," I counter. "It's where I belong, not going to change."

"You're not helping with the insults, Ashley," Camron snipes. "Blake, will you at least let me show you the new business before you just write us off again?"

"That's why I'm here." Among other things. They haven't presented me with the real reason for this ride yet. I should've suspected they'd find someone to do their dirty work though.

"Good. Let's enjoy the scenery or you can tell me about your girl on the way to the resort that your parents are building and need to check on. They need our input on a few things, and I'd like to meet the new additions to the family while I'm here."

"*Our* input? I don't think so, Camron."

If this is the family gathering that the mother convened, to convince me we're tight-knit, she'll have to do better, if that's possible. "How many businesses are we going to visit? I have to get back to Astrid and my son. The farther I get away from them the sicker I feel." I'm not lying—nausea is active in my esophagus and promising to make my breakfast reappear.

"We're going to only one, Blake. Why can't I meet them?"

"I don't want them any more tainted with the dynamic of this family than they already are. I hate to contaminate the high and mighty Powers with Astrid's brown skin, her middle-class upbringing, and job. She's someone this family isn't willing to acknowledge as human with feelings. You're a Powers too, Camron."

He winces. I think I hurt *his* feelings.

"That's enough disrespect, Blake," the father speaks up. Now, where was his spine when I was growing up?

"Is it really, father? I'm failing to see why I should listen to anything you say when you tried to alienate the woman I love last night before she could give the impression she wanted anything to do with you, denied my child before he's even born, and didn't bother to come inside while Dr. Ellis was releasing me. But the mother was pretty vocal about getting me placed in her care like I'm two years old, for easy contact to fool me into believing things that this family isn't capable of. You're always all in for whatever your wife wants. This isn't a family. This is a circus, and she's the ringleader. Am I wrong?"

"I didn't deny or alienate anyone, Blake," he defends.

"That's right. You stood behind *her* and let her do all the ranting and name-calling. You're just guilty by association. That sounds so much better. I should've never gotten in this car."

Animosity wafts off the mother, as she crosses her legs beneath a black, calf-length skirt. "I will apologize to your little girlfriend if you at least go with us to the site."

"The little girlfriend has a name. Astrid, and she doesn't need you to apologize, especially since you'll only be doing it to placate me. She's not rich, but she's not stupid either."

"Still, I'll apologize."

"Why?"

"Because the further I push her away, the further you run. The Owens have already stolen your loyalty from us. The least you could do is let us work on getting it back before running back to *her*."

"The least I can do is forgive you two for throwing parties and raising money for my sister that isn't here while ignoring your son his whole life. *That's* how you lost my loyalty. And now that I'm grown, I'm of some use to you. I won't let you use me like that. Stuff your business in—"

"Blake!" Camron yells.

Yeah, I may have been about to take it too far, but my shoulders feel lighter. I understand why I offered to see them today; needed to purge my system of the baggage I've been carrying around since I was a little boy that loved his parents even when they were oblivious to what he needed.

"Camron, I didn't ask them to make me live in the shadow of my sister, and I wished she had lived. Maybe, I would've had someone to love me back in their household. I don't regret the parties they threw in her honor though because they brought me parents that loved me like their own, and the sister I didn't have would become Malisa. I got what I needed, and it didn't come at a cost."

The father grimaces. "You have your memories back then?"

I almost mistake his question as true interest.

"Yes, I do." I want to call Astrid badly, just not with the company I'm in. They're so toxic they could pollute her mood over the phone and dilute the good news.

His crossed hands in his lap become captivating. "When?"

"Do you care?"

He looks me directly in the eyes for the first time in years. "Yes." Damn, I believe him this time, but the mother will annihilate his concern quickly. He'll let her.

"They came back just in time. That's all you need to know."

"Blake, we can't repair our broken relationship if you don't let us in."

He opens a door that I'm tempted to put my foot in. The father isn't as much the bad guy as the mother is.

"Does repairing include running your businesses?"

"Not for me, Prince, no." So, he hasn't forgotten the nickname he used to call me before the mother shut it down when he was getting too close to his own son.

"Martin!" she howls. "Don't encourage him not to take over his responsibilities!"

"Well, there's her answer that no one solicited," I state sarcastically, with a grin. "The Power's empire isn't my responsibility. It's whoever started it, all for the prestige and power that they bring for the family. And you need someone to keep that alive. I'm an afterthought. You've missed all the things that count in life which is why you can't give it. You'll be begging for it on your death bed. You won't get it because father will be throwing a party for his deceased daughter just like you taught him to do."

She clutches her damn pearls. "You take that back, Blake."

"Why? It's the truth. What you denied me will be exactly what you need on your dying day? Until then, you'll continue to be the dragon that burns up everything good around you. And I'm fine with that. I've made my peace with it. You should too. I'm getting out at the next stop. It hasn't been fabulous talking with you all. Have a good life anyway."

"Just wait a minute, Blake," Camron pleads. "You haven't given me a chance to do better by our family relations, and I do wish we were tighter cousins. It's time-consuming to run a business, which is why you haven't seen me. I haven't left Candleton since I started my business there, so at least spend some time with *me* if not your parents. I didn't even get to meet Astrid, so you don't know how I'll treat her, which will be as if she's a human with feelings because she's important to you. All you have to do is let me prove it. Little Blake should get to know someone from his father's side anyway. It'll be a privilege if it was me."

Dragon lady puffs up. "Camron, I didn't bring you here for this." The shutting down of all things good is in progress.

"No, you didn't, Aunt Ashley, but you can't control me anymore than you can Blake. That's what this is about. Control, and apparently, you're not getting it, so let it go. I'll still show Blake the resort because I keep my promises, but I want to be a part of his new family even if you don't. I'm going to if he lets me."

Well, I'll be damn. Camron, the billionaire playboy, may be outgrowing his family's vigorous training of how the world show bow down to him while he takes it by the horns. His parents raised him the way mine tried to do to me. He fell in line with what they wanted after he grew up, increasing the Powers' legacy by starting an umbrella company under the parent company in Italy that his parents still run. He didn't have the Owens to open his eyes, so I can show at least him some compassion. It's the right thing to do, until it isn't.

"Fine, Camron. We'll tour the construction site, but not with them. I've had all I can take of these Powers. In one hour, I'm going back to Astrid."

"Blake," she begins.

Father seizes her elbow. "Let it go, Ashley. You've done enough damage."

"What? Martin, you don't speak to me that way. What has gotten into you?"

He looks at me for a moment. "Some sense. We'll drop them off and send the car back for them. You and I need to talk at home, Ashley, and it's past time for it. You are so not going to like this conversation."

Father putting his feet down? Shit just got entertaining. I cross my arms and get comfortable in my seat, predicting fireworks from the dragon lady.

Camron shakes his head. "Blake, do you have a picture of Astrid?"

I scrounge for my phone, prompt the screensaver while the parents hiss words at each other like cobras.

Camron examines her picture, gets melancholic as if he's thinking of someone who's too far away, then returns the phone. "She's beautiful. I'd like to meet her today, if you're okay with it."

"She is beautiful, eight months pregnant, and I should be with her right now instead of dealing with this. You are welcome to meet her if it's okay with her. If it isn't, she'll let us know. Trust me."

"Well, I'm glad you came. We had some good times as kids. Hopefully, we'll pick up where we left off." It's more like we got cut off, by the dragon lady.

"We did have good times, Camron. We must have been getting too close."

He nods slowly. "I think that's what the Powers do best, corrupt. They damn sure got your mother good. She forgot she's from the back side of Spindle."

Now, that's breaking news, everyone. "How did I not know this?" I ask, thoroughly intrigued.

She freaks out, flailing her arms. "Why the hell did you tell him that, Camron?"

He laughs. "She never meant for you to find out, Blake. That's how you didn't know."

"I'm right here!" she shouts. "I haven't been *from* Spindle in thirty years!"

Father rucks up his lips. "That's the problem, Ashley, you forgot your roots and I let you. Now, my son hates me."

I take a good look at the mother. All her prestige and power, she inherited by marriage. I never thought about how she obtained it, so it never occurred to me that she had to carve a niche into the Powers and society—she just seemed to fit right in to a little boy that never knew any different. I think my father is about to demolish the life she's made after leaving everyone behind… in Spindle. I bet I have family there too, and it's sad I never knew they existed before now.

The car slows down, and I prepare to let myself out. The atmosphere in the immaculate car is completely unclean with the dirt that's been swept from under rugs that have been nailed down. Camron lets himself out on the other side. Steel beams challenge the height of the mountains in the distance, jutting out of framework nowhere near to being finished, several hundred feet back from the road that we begin following. White bricks are partially covering the first three floors, the only ones that have walls. My gut starts to eat on itself.

"Why are we really here, Camron?" I ask cagily.

"You know why." He puts his hands in his pockets.

"This is supposed to be my umbrella company, isn't it?"

I don't need a response. The secret's out.

"Yep, ten floors for the elite to sun themselves under artificial lights, eat hundred-dollar dinner plates with not enough to food to fill up a puppy, and drink wine and champagne that cost more than I pay my personal assistant every month. She's here by the way with some of that wine on the first floor. We were supposed to have brunch with your parents here and discuss who would design the interior. The supposedly great ones must be booked a year in advance, and you would approve a budget for that and negotiate your CEO salary. It would've started at one million a year, topped out at two. The first number you picked is what you were going to be stuck with until this place was in the black. You also needed to decide what to do with the contracted construction company. As you can see, no one is here working, and they've fallen behind. Ashley thinks they're ripping us off and she wanted you to—"

"To whip them into shape or let them go."

"Correct. Being a businessman is in your blood, Blake."

"I choose not to utilize it. Why are you still endorsing for the parents?"

"As of right now, I'm endorsing for Astrid and your son. Shouldn't you take every opportunity to *give* them opportunities? Only money can do that, but I'm not saying you have to conform to your parents' every want, or even enter their circle. It's not like you'll be using your parents for what they have to take care of your family. Ashley and Martin are literally trying to throw you down and make you take a better life that you can shape how you want to. It doesn't hurt that you have a career to fall back on if they get out of hand with the manipulating. I don't have a plan

B, like a law enforcement career, and it's the stupidest thing I ever done. I think."

He has a point; Astrid deserves a castle, too. "You forgetting the parents don't want my choice of family near theirs. I'm not leaving Astrid and my son behind for anyone. The parents will insist on that. Trust me."

"Your mother will, but your father seems to be jumping ship, which leaves your mother power*less*. Technically, the companies are his, and they have a prenup. She gets nothing if he divorces her. If they want you to take a company for yourself so badly, sounds like your family is a serious bargaining chip, isn't it?"

"They are but Astrid wants nothing to do with them. I wouldn't make anyone deal with the dragon lady and her sidekick."

Camron laughs and enters the opening in the first floor that will be the front entry for the resort, one day. "I think Astrid would deal with them for you, and from what I heard about her, she's pretty damn good at putting the dragon lady and her sidekick in their places. Ashley was furious when she called me last night. Did Astrid really tell Ashley that Martin should make her eat a sandwich?"

"Yes, and the arguing was stressful for Astrid. She's a sweet woman with a matching nature, and no one is going to make her unhappy."

"You're extremely protective of her, so make sure everyone gets along by not having them in the same room ever. Do you really want the dragon lady anywhere near your son after her history with you?" Or his parents' history with him. Money seems to make for bad parenting skills in this family.

"Not even in the slightest, Camron."

"There you go then. Amari!"

Footsteps emanate at the back of the building with free-standing barriers sprouting up from the floor. Zig-zagging around them is a slender woman with caramel-skin, an hour-glass figure, and flats below her tan skirt suit. She stops in front of Camron, peering up at him with the same evil eye I was bestowing on my bullet vest.

"Yes, Mr. Powers." Her tone could cut glass.

The wistfulness that Camron displayed while looking at Astrid's picture sloshes off him in currents.

He's got a thing for his assistant.

"Meet Blake Powers. Blake, Amari Spencer. You can pack up everything but two glasses of champagne, Amari. Bring them while we wait for the car. The brunch is cancelled and we'll be leaving shortly. Hurry up."

Her dark eyes train on me and snap at us both now, though, I can see the relief in hers as well. She does not want to be here. Me either, and Camron is her reason why. He's an idiot.

"Nice to meet you, Mr. Powers."

Yeah, well, I don't think so, thanks to Camron's rude ass.

"Nice to meet you too, Mrs. Spencer. I can help you with packing if you need it."

Her face opens up with her astonishment. "Uh, no, but thank you. This is my job. I'll be right back with your champagne, and it's just Amari. I'm not married." She goes back the way she came.

When she's out of sight, Camron whirls around on me. "Why in the world did you offer to help her, Blake?"

"Why *didn't* you?"

"Because I pay her to be my assistant, so she assists, which is following orders, and I pay her very damn well for it. Oh, and I want to extend an invitation to you and Astrid. You guys should come visit me in New York. I'll even spring for the plane tickets and hotel. I don't care about Astrid and the baby being who they are."

"No, you wouldn't care, Camron, not with the way you keep looking at your personal assistant." Who loathes him, but I'm not one to gossip. "I'll ask Astrid if she wants to visit you after she meets you."

"She'll want to visit me, Blake."

I chuckle. "Why? Because you're you?"

He grins, his ego sitting on his left shoulder like a miniature devil. "Well yes, of course."

I take it back. Pompous Camron hasn't changed; everyone is still here to fulfill his wishes. He's been ruined. Since I know where to place the blame for that and he's not prejudiced like the parents, I laugh at him.

"Get over yourself, Camron."

His lips widen. "Why in the hell would I do that?"

Amari brings back the champagne. She smiles and distributes a flute to me first. "Thank you, Amari."

"You're welcome, Mr. Powers."

"Call me Blake."

"Will do, Blake."

When she hands over Camron's, they're both frowning. Amari double-times it out of there. I clink my glass against his.

"You get over yourself, Camron, so you can stop mooning over your assistant. You'll never get her with that 'thy is your king' attitude your parents taught you. She's your equal, looking for a man with manners to walk beside not behind. 'Please' and 'thank you' go a long way towards building relationships. Money only gets you an employee, but don't listen to me. I'm just a Sheriff in a small town with not much money in the bank."

He's all eyes for Amari's backside that's *been* out of sight. "We can change the balance of your bank account, Blake, but you've got to give something to get something better."

Better? As if what I have isn't good enough. Now, I'm pissy.

"Don't make me feel ungrateful for what I've worked my ass off for, Camron. No, I don't have millions in the bank, but I pay my bills ahead of time every month, and can afford to raise a family and give them everything they need."

"Well, I want you to give them the world. A sheriff's salary isn't going to cut it. After your term is up, and you don't get re-elected, what then? Are you going to take a pay cut and work as a deputy? Or move to another town and run for sheriff there? You can float from job to job when you're single. This resort is stability, exactly what Astrid and your son will need for their lifetime." They don't need the Powers.

"Camron, if it was any other family, I could take your advice. The Powers are cutthroat, self-important, and uppity. Those are their best qualities."

"Change has to start with someone, and giving Ashley and Martin the cold-shoulder only draws them to you. Your parents will leave you alone if you do this. You can give your family everything. This place already has a clientele because the snobs are followers and the Powers are leaders. Whatever else Ashley and Martin demand of you, you just refuse. It's been working so far because you have your dream job and your girl. The best part is I can teach you what you don't know about the business so you don't run it into the ground while I beat your ass at poker."

I'll be damned if his subtle arm-twisting isn't working. Being out of a job, if the next election doesn't pan out, won't be a problem. The baby's college fund won't have to be saved a few pennies at a time. Astrid can live anywhere she wants to. She won't have to work if she chooses. I'll provide like I'm supposed to.

"First off, you can quit with the jokes, Camron. You don't have the attention span required to beat me at cards. Second, I'll have to talk to Astrid. If she isn't with this, neither am I.

"Good man. Call her now. Set up the brunch at the station so we can chat and eat." He downs his drink then eyeballs the empty flute. "Amari! Bring the rest of the champagne! Change of plans! We're eating at the sheriff's department! That's going to be interesting!" He walks off. "Are you done packing yet? The car's coming soon! What is taking you so long, woman?"

Poor Amari.

Poor Camron. He'll have the money without the girl until the day he dies or he changes. One is much more likely than the other, and I pity him, but he is damn entertaining.

****

Astrid

The scribbling on my notepad stops when my phone rings in the bottom drawer of Blake's desk. I don't care if it's a telemarketer calling, I'm answering. It's just too lonely in the station without Blake livening up the place with his personality. Meagan's daughter is still sick, so she's homebound. Councilman Alder has been long gone, sticking around long enough to inquire about my plan for getting Blake back in uniform, how many more deputies I'll need during my time as acting Sheriff, and to present me with a maternity-sized uniform he had shipped overnight. Copper is on patrol all day since there's no one else to do it.

Blake's name scrolls across my screen.

I swipe the accept icon too hard and fumble the phone. "Hey, baby. Are you okay?"

"I'm fine, love. Why are you breathing so hard? I need to talk to you about something."

There isn't supposed to be anything to talk about, unless... the Powers have got their hooks in him.

A throb shoots between my eyebrows. My heart takes a header into my stomach, which skydives into my black clogs. My grip on the phone slackens. It clatters onto the desktop face up.

"Astrid!" The earpiece evicts his anguish. "Baby!"

"I'm here. Just wait, Blake."

I aim for the speakerphone button and punch the mute instead. Several times, I try with bloodless fingertips and miss, damn near have dialed another number before I hit the right icon.

"What are you doing, Astrid?"

"Nothing, just say what you have to, so I can make some calls before the rental offices close. And call my parents to have them send my furniture from Harrison." All missions impossible if I'm still numb after this conversation is over.

"Rental? Sweetheart, it's not what you think! I want to do this face to face and introduce you to someone."

What?

"Who?"

"My cousin."

"He's a Powers too, isn't he?" Which means another altercation with his family. *Fuck!*

"Yes, he's family. Just meet him, hear what we have to say then decide if our plan is something you can live with." Good God. What are they up to? Can't be anything good if they need to talk to me.

"I don't want to have to live without you, Blake." I will if he wants me to associate with his people.

Yes, my existence will amount to simply taking up space on the planet and overcompensating with Little Blake for failing to keep Blake in our lives, but it's better than going toe to toe with bigots every time I'm in their crosshairs. Been there. Done that. Got the T-shirt, and burned that bitch when I put Harrison in my rearview mirror three years ago, sick of the prejudice.

"You won't have to live without me ever, Astrid, no matter what you decide. Now, take a break, please. I'm down the street. Meet me outside the station."

"Bye." I don't attempt to hang up before bounding out of his chair, going outside.

Chapter Fifteen

Astrid

The bright morning light predicts a gorgeous day. Might as well be grey and cloudy. In the graveled lot, I pace in front of my truck, grill reflecting in the department's glass door that I tumbled out of on tingling feet, until a limo is crunching the rocks beneath its tires. No point in talking to Blake now, I know what he wants to discuss; living like the Powers. It's already started for him with the suits and chauffeurs. Next will come the jet-setting to exotic locations. Might as well be another galaxy for those with lesser breeding and only eight thousand dollars to their name. I can see them now, the tendrils attaching to Blake, drawing him away until we're passing ships in the night. Eventually, one of us won't come back. I won't let our love decline to disposable. Better to set him free now while he's still the man I fell for.

I freeze, searching out my Blake, before he becomes theirs and unrecognizable. Both back doors swing wide on the car. Blond and dark hair eclipse the car on each side until similar faces are visible. On their way to me, both men are suited and booted, undiscovered male models, gavel clumping under their soles. It's almost too much damn testosterone incoming, even outdoors where the atmosphere should be watering it down.

Outnumbered, I claw at my elbows, while I splinter inside.

Ashley and Martin called in reinforcements to fight a war against little old me. Waste of their time. I'm not going to be a hurdle that Blake must jump, repeatedly, because they can't accept me. He shouldn't be put through this. Somebody has to be willing to do what's best for him. Let them be the obstacles he needs to get around to see his son. I had Blake for a little while, and that'll have to be enough.

When Blake towers over me, he caresses my upturned cheek. "Are you going to hear me out first?"

"Y-yes." Stuttering makes it seem as if I'm asking.

The mystery relative flanks my right. Insults maybe being sharpened on the tip of his well-bred palate. I'm not going down without a fight even if the Powers have already won. They can't have my dignity too.

Blake kidnaps my hands in his, incarcerating them in his chest, against his steady heartbeat. "Camron from New York, originally from Italy, meet Astrid Daniels from Utah. Astrid, Camron."

"Hello, Astrid." Traces of an accent fading tinge his baritone. No doubt it drives the women crazy. Then, Camron kisses my cheek.

What the hell?

Wondering what game is he playing, I stare at him clueless, waiting for him to say something belittling.

"Keep your lips to your damn self, Camron." Blake growls.

Camron grins, then winks. Blake's head crooks to the side. His tongue laps at the nook in my lips. Automatically, I gun for his mouth, and go up in flames, or I'm going down. Senses have already crashed. I can't distinguish which direction I'm heading in.

You didn't even try to save yourself.

Can't with Blake's mouth wreaking havoc. Jesus, he's seducing me right in front of his cousin. Supposed to be backing off so he doesn't have far to go to leave me behind.

Then pull back, up, or something.

Right.

Breathless, I disconnect. "It's okay, Blake. You don't have to choose..." Cracking in my voice takes my ability to speak. "...between me and your family anymore. You never should've had to. I bow out gracefully, but I'm not moving back to Harrison. Come see the baby when you want to." It's not like I'll have another man. Who can compare to Blake anyway?

No one, but you're on the end of the open alligator's mouth too when it comes to who compares to living a lavish lifestyle.

Touché, conscience.

Blake's lips swoop down for a swift peck, leaving singe marks on my mouth and me wanting more. "You're supposed to hear me out first, baby, remember?"

"I'm listening."

"Open your eyes then."

I didn't know they were closed. "Sorry."

Camron chuckles.

Blake's baby blues dwell into the heart of me. "Castle, private jet, little princes, and princesses running around, destroying things. The option for you to stay at home with them or start your own business and set your own hours. Me coming home to *your* kingdom every evening. Unlimited opportunities for the babies to choose between or take advantage of everything this world has to offer. Those are the things I want to give you, Astrid. Being a sheriff isn't going to provide that, not when my job runs out every four years. It's not guaranteed I'll get into office again, but struggling until I find another sheriff's job that pays as much as this one is for sure."

"You love this job, Blake."

His hands encompass my belly; his brow lowers to mine. "I love my family more, and working in the established Powers' businesses is how I can give it everything. Do this with me, Astrid. I can't do it without you."

"You and the baby are the only thing I need, Blake. I don't want you sacrificing for me, and I can't be bumping heads with your parents every time I—"

"They won't come anywhere near us. They're not allowed to. It's you, me, our babies, and one high-end resort that I run. Two million a year. Whatever your heart desires. There'll be no sacrifices on either end if you're standing beside me."

"What if you're miserable at a job you're taking because you want to give me material things?"

A hand drops down on my shoulder. Camron's. "Blake won't be miserable, Astrid. He'll have me and you. You and baby Blake will have me too. Just think of me as the great wall. The rest of the Powers on one side. Your family on the other."

I squint up at Camron. "You're only one man. You can't hold them all off from New York. Why would you? You don't know me."

"Because you make my cousin truly happy. The Powers need shining examples of that." Camron scratches at the back of his head and looks out toward the limo for a second. "So do I. We don't usually bother each other if each is making money for the empire. There's the annual trip where we all descend on Italy just to discuss the branch companies' finances with my parents. The Powers' men don't usually pick women with maternal instincts, so Ashley won't be stopping by to see her grandchildren or Blake as long as she thinks he's doing what she wants. I'll tell Ashley myself to stay away from your home, unless she wants Blake to cut her off again. He knows how to say no to anything else he doesn't want to do, or he wouldn't have you in the first place, and dammit, I'm fun to be around. And I do say so myself." Can one man really be so cocky?

"How do you fit your head through doorways?"

"I build bigger doorways, which is why I'm in real estate, and I'll be scouting architects for your castle. I know all the best ones."

My castle with the man I love as king, I like it.

"So you'll be coming around, Camron?" I don't trust him as far as I can throw him.

That's not saying much, Astrid. You're trained in self-defense.

Okay, I trust him about as much as I can see him with my eyes closed then. Can I deal with one Powers to make Blake happy? Damn straight, when he needs me as much as I do him, and I'll just kick Camron's ass if he gets out of line.

"Okay, I'm in."

Blake arms constrict around me. Camron embraces us both and jiggles us around. My nose smashes against somebody's arm. "I can't breathe, people."

Camron backs off.

Blake doesn't. "Sorry, baby. I admit Camron's a lot of fun though. I told you I got into a lot of trouble as a kid. He was worse. Now, he's a damn train wreck waiting to happen as an adult. You'll enjoy seeing him get his comeuppance though, and you won't believe what form it's coming in. Or maybe you will."

That can only mean one thing. "A woman."

"Amari Spencer. Brown skin, smurf-size, giant attitude, has manners, and knows an impolite idiot when she works for one."

"Blake, you're not supposed to discuss my feelings with your soon-to-be-wife," Camron rebukes. "You just tossed the bro-code right out the window."

I laugh. "You should've brought Amari here." The enemy of my... not sure if Camron's an enemy yet, but I'll still make her my friend anyway.

"She's in the car," Blake informs, highly amused. "Want to meet her?"

My eyebrow jacks up. "You left her in the *car*?"

He pitches a thumb over his shoulder at Camron. "*He* left her in the car. Ill-mannered bastard."

"Sticks and stones, Blake," Camron wisecracks.

"Well, get her out, somebody," I scold.

"I'll do it." Camron retraces his steps to the car. "Amari! Get out already! With the food! I'm hungry!"

Lord!

I tune out Camron, going to be doing that a lot. "When were you going to tell me that you got your memories back, Blake?"

"When we finished discussing the rest of our lives."

"Well, I know you're not supposed to be driving, cooking, skiing, swimming, using heavy equipment, and working, for at least a week."

"How do you know I'm not supposed to be doing anything but breathing and sleeping if Dr. Ellis gets his way?"

"I called him after Councilman Alder left, to check on you and get the details of your release. Did you think I wouldn't?"

"Actually, I didn't think about it, love, because it never occurred to me that you wouldn't care, which is why I couldn't wait to get back to you. You can drive us home if you want to. Me and my son haven't talked all day. Well, I talk and he kicks. Same thing."

"Blake, you've been gone an hour. That is *not* all day... but I'm damn glad it feels like it to you."

"It always will, Astrid, so get use to me cyber-stalking you when I'm at work. I'm going to need pictures of the baby and several 'I love yous' back."

"Done." I tilt his chin downward.

"Don't you two start kissing!" Camron cock blocks, on his way back. "Nobody else is doing it!" And he's irked about it too.

A very attractive woman carries a massive basket, stumbling over the gravel and catapulting daggers at Camron's back with midnight black eyes whenever her shoulder-length, jet-black hair isn't swinging into them.

"Oh, she definitely hates him, Blake. Love is *not* going to come easy for those two."

"Well, he's promised to stay in contact. Wants us to visit him in New York soon and he'll come to Colorado more often, so we'll have lots of chances to convert him into a decent man, Astrid."

"We hope."

A month later

Blake

Long exhales of my name and whispered moans disturb the edges of my sleep until I roll toward the origin of them, drowsily, finding Astrid asleep on her side. A hand is tucked between her thighs, the other cradling her head. Her ass cheeks, round as two full moons, gyrate against my hard-on.

God, she is killing me.

Blake Jr., or BJ, is only three weeks old, with three more to go before Astrid can resume sex and go back to work as acting Sheriff.

Evidently, she can't wait that long if she's pleasuring herself while unconscious.

I gently jostle her into a prone position, spread her legs apart slowly then kneel between them. It's fucking sexy to watch her masturbate by early morning light that's blitzing the room with slivers of its luminosity falling across her body. Giving her what she wants the most will give me so much more pleasure. I grab her wrist lightly and remove it to her flat stomach with little gray streaks on it. She groans, displeased with my meddling.

Placing my hands in the bends of her thighs, I lap at her clitoris. Her legs seal shut around my neck, like a noose. When she's quivering and her juices are coating my chin, I walk up the bed on my hands and knees and slide an inch into her with controlled enthusiasm. I could drive into her with one stroke since she's so damn wet, but she's still healing and I'm damn sure not about to hinder that.

Her knees coast into the air as I work myself unhurriedly deeper into her depths. A lengthy breath filled with satisfaction blows softly out of her lips. Her head starts to thrash around on the pillow, her hands grabbing for my waist to hold on to something solid. My anchor is her pillow cocooning my hands.

I withdraw, and a whiny sound dispels from her tiny nostrils. She's unhappy again. I can't have that, so I swing forward until every inch of my rod is lost in her. She smiles sluggishly then grabs two handfuls of my ass, holding me in place. Her muscles start to contract and release, milking the base of my length. *Good God.*

If she keeps this up, it'll be over in a matter of seconds, after I barrel into her like an eighteen-wheeler. Jerking backwards, taking half of my length with me, I begin a short, pumping rhythm, hitting her g-spot and nothing more. She lifts her hips, seeking the bottoming out of my cock in her. Begrudging her, I draw my knees under her thighs so she can't ambush me, while she gasps from the exquisite torture I know I'm laying down. I can't give her what she wants the most without hurting her, and that's all of me. I can damn sure deliver what she was hunting for in her dreams; an orgasm. At least two to make up for what she can't have.

"Blake, please," she begs, for me to slam into her.

"No, sweetheart, you can't handle that right now. And I'll only fuck you harder if I give in to you."

Astrid caves in on herself suddenly, her knees digging into my diaphragm. The clenching and releasing of her muscles rockets up my need to cum. Lightning bolts electrocute my spine. A blinding climax that would bring me to my knees if I wasn't laying down, dislodges. Too damn intense to withstand, I crawl up the bed on my elbows, going deeper into her slowly, needing to escape the avalanche raining down on me.

A cry splits the air wide open. The blonde-hair, hazel-eyed, eight-pound boss in a diaper is awake next door in his nursery. I smack Astrid on the mouth before emptying her body. "Sleep, baby. I got him."

She doesn't argue. I rescue my robe from the floor and snatch my phone off the nightstand. After taking an immediate right, I pick up the baby boy who quiets down immediately. I confess it's much more fun interacting with him outside the womb. Astrid and I have had several friendly disagreements about if he's smiling or just gassy when I'm talking to him.

Quickly changing his diaper, we stash a bottle in the warmer in the kitchen. I dial Camron, who's awake at six in the morning, at the office, where he often sleeps in a hidden bedroom built behind a wall.

"Camron, did you get it?"

"Morning to you too, Blake. And no, I didn't get it."

"Why not?" This is what I get for letting Camron be my accomplice.

"Because your mother got it."

"Who?

"Your mother. I told her what I was doing for you so Astrid didn't catch wind of it before the big day. Ashley took it upon herself to pay for Astrid's ring I had designed, had an extra carat added, secured a vineyard upstate for the surprise engagement party, and is currently taking care of the menu and the guest list. Every person she and you know will be there. And I mean every damn one. The Owens. The Daniels. Friends. And... the Powers."

Good goddamn.

"Astrid is going to have a stroke. Why didn't you tell me this before now?"

"Because I think your mother has honorable intentions for once in her life. I thought she did a pretty damn good job of getting all of this done with just phone calls from hundreds of miles away. I hadn't prepared for the hell you were going to raise yet, and I can't see Astrid denying an older lady her last wishes after giving your father a chance to be a part of his grandson's life." He's forgetting Astrid was in an extremely joyful mood, welcoming her son to the world, when my father arrived at the hospital with a sincere apology for Ashley mistreating her, and wanting to be a better father and grandfather. We haven't seen hide nor hair of the mother since my hospital stay.

"What do you mean an older lady's last wishes?"

"Well, something's wrong with Ashley. Something has to be. She's being nice, or she's jealous since Martin's allowed to spoil BJ and she isn't. I haven't pinned down the reason yet, but she wants to apologize to Astrid publicly at the party and be the first to welcome her into the family officially. I think you should give them a chance to work things out between them."

"I keep hearing 'you think'. What I'm going to do is take the surprise out of the engagement party. I'm not letting Astrid walk in there unprepared. And Camron, if Astrid divorces me before she even marries me, I'm killing you for it. You were not supposed to let the mother take over."

"It's fine, Blake," Astrid says from behind me, spooking the hell out of me.

I whirl around. "Jesus, woman!"

She giggles and tests the bottle before feeding BJ in my arms. "You should turn the volume down on your phone's speaker and your dial pad. My hearing is like a superpower now that BJ is here. Your mother coming to the engagement party is fine. What kind of woman would I be if I hold grudges and exclude someone because of who they are? That's the type of crap that had me moving to Arrow, and would make me a hypocrite. There's enough of those in the world. People do change. And if there's a chance you can have everyone in your life who should be in it, then who am I to put up roadblocks?"

"The Powers are not going to be the same after you, baby." Maybe Camron did the right thing letting the dragon lady in where Astrid and I wouldn't.

"We can hope, sweetheart, but I haven't forgotten my self-defense training. If anyone of your family members comes at me sideways, you've been warned."

Camron cracks up on the phone. "I'll be at this party with bells on."

"Bye, Camron." I lay the phone down on the counter beside Astrid's hip. "I hung up so I can steal a kiss from you in peace. You are my everything, you know that?"

With the remaining hand, I entomb it in her hair and slowly draw her close.

"Ditto. Now, why steal kisses when they're yours already, Blake?"

"Are they?"

"Every single damn one, from the moment you opened your office door and slammed it back shut on my first day as your deputy."

The End... For Now.

Read more of the *hearts on the line* saga of the powerful men who love with their whole hearts from a distance with Camron and Amari's Story in **Undisclosed Desire 3: The Contracted Lovers.**

Available Now